They've got to get out.

"Let's just get someplace safe and comfortable. I'll tell you everything. I owe you that much."

"Got that right." Another horrible thought crossed her mind. "If the house isn't safe, what about the others? My friends?"

"They've got to get out too," Daniel replied. "As quickly as possible. Are they at the house now?"

"Some of them, maybe . . ."

"You've got to warn them," he said. "Get them away from there."

"What am I supposed to tell them? I'm in the dark here, remember?"

"We'll find a safe pl_____ ___ mised. "When we do, ju__ ____ _____ ___ us there—witho_____ _____ ____ ___ re they're going_____ _____ ____matic, but their lives ___ _____ _ now."

He took on_____ ___ the steering wheel and squeezed he_____ left shoulder. "Kerry, I truly am sorry you got involved in this. If I could undo it, I would."

Kerry shrugged, and he took his hand away. "Yeah, well, that makes two of us."

As the seasons change, so does Kerry. . . .
Check out the next installments
in the Witch Season series:

Fall

Winter

Spring

Coming soon from Simon Pulse

witch
season

SUMMER

JEFF MARIOTTE

Simon Pulse
New York London Toronto Sydney

This one's for Lisa.

Copyright © 2004 by Jeff Mariotte
First Simon Pulse edition July 2004

SIMON PULSE
An imprint of Simon & Schuster
Children's Publishing Division
1230 Avenue of the Americas
New York, NY 10020

Designed by Ann Sullivan
The text of this book was set in Bembo.

Printed in the United States of America
10 9 8 7 6 5 4 3 2 1

Library of Congress Control Number 2003114111

ISBN 0-689-86665-8

Special thanks to Amanda Berger; Howard Morhaim and Mara Sorkin; Tara O'Shea; Cindy Chapman; and my family, Maryelizabeth, Holly, and David.

Kerry Profitt's diary, August 11

Once again I woke up screaming. Drenched in sweat, wet sheets tangled around my legs as if I'd been flailing them for hours. Brandy even came into our room and told me she could tell the instant I snapped out of it. My mouth was open like a gasping fish, she said, and then it closed, and my eyes opened. And I had let out a real ear-piercer, because, after all, there was this face in front of me, looking at me like I was some kind of sideshow freak.

Which, you know, if the shoe fits . . .

When my heart stopped trying to tear through my rib cage, and I could breathe again, she asked me what I'd been dreaming about. Hell if I know, I told her. Whenever I wake up, I can never remember anything more than an overpowering sense of dread. Doom on wheels.

Maybe it's the weird hours I've been keeping. I worked till eleven last night, same as the night before, but had the breakfast-and-lunch shift for three days before that. Today it's the late shift again, so I slept in probably longer than I should have. My head is throbbing so hard I can barely see the computer screen, and who knows if I'll be able to read this later?

But that's why Einstein invented ibuprofen, right? And spell check. And Scott's brewing fresh coffee. Nectar of the gods.

More later.

K.

1

She couldn't see the ocean from where she stood on a grease-caked cement step just outside the kitchen's back door. A row of bungalows—identical dark boxes, some with glowing windows—blocked her view. She could hear the water, though—the steady, dull thunder of the surf reminding her that it was close, at the edge of both the Seaside Resort and the continent. And she could smell it, a sharp tang that battled for supremacy over the smells of steak, seafood, and smoke that blew out from the kitchen. Towering above the bungalows, underlit by the resort's floodlights, incredibly tall palm trees swayed on their skinny trunks in the evening breeze, looking like skyrocket bursts frozen in time at the ends of their own contrails. A sliver of crescent moon dangled above them, high and distant.

Kerry Profitt was a daughter of the great plains, born and raised near the confluence of two great rivers in Cairo, Illinois. But the Mississippi and Ohio, powerful as they were, had nothing on the Pacific Ocean. The ocean was magical to her, its depths and mysteries were boundless, its call irresistible. She had made a point, since hitting La Jolla, California, for her summer job, of keeping it in sight whenever possible. Bad for the skin, all that sun and salt air, and she, with her complexion like fresh snow ("whitest white girl I've ever seen" was what Brandy said) knew better. But she couldn't deny the ocean's magnetic pull.

Lost in thought, she didn't see the shadowed figure slip into the alley, didn't know she wasn't alone until the voice startled her. "Hey, Kerr, where is it the swallows go back to?"

Startled, she managed to keep her cool, and she smiled when she recognized the voice. She knew it belonged to Josh Quinn, one of her housemates, but it took her a moment to refocus her gaze and pick him out in the dark alley. His skin was every bit as pale as hers, but by choice, not genetics, and the black of his hair came from a bottle, unlike hers. He looked as out-of-place in the valet's uniform—white shirt, maroon vest, black pants—as a lion on a kindergarten playground.

"Umm . . . Capistrano, I think," Kerry replied after a moment's consideration. She was used to this kind of thing from Josh, king of the nonsequitur. *If his middle name isn't Random, it should be.*

"Yeah, that's right," he agreed.

Since it didn't seem like he was going to take the discussion any further, she decided to press the point. "Why?"

He struck a match in the darkness and shielded it with cupped hands to a cigarette held between his lips. "These tourists, man," he said around the butt. Then, blowing out a plume of smoke—away from Kerry, because she would have killed him if he hadn't—he continued with an exasperated tone. "They're like those swallows."

"The ones in Capistrano?"

"Yeah, those."

"In what way?" *You had to ask,* she immediately chastised herself, bracing for the answer.

"Some of them seem to come here every summer, like clockwork."

She had noticed the same thing, though without the bird metaphor. "Good for business, I guess," she pointed out.

"I guess. But this one guy—you know the kind, enormous gut, Texas accent, gold watch that cost more than everything I've owned in my life put together—yelled at me just now because I didn't turn on the heat in his Mercedes."

"The heat?" Kerry asked with surprise. It was a fairly cool night. They all were here, close to the water, and balmy eves, she had learned, were not so much a southern California thing. Once the sun went down, the day's heat fled fast. But even so, far from wintry cold.

"That's what I said. Only it was more like, 'Dude, are you freaking crazy? It's August!' And he was like, 'I told you last year, if it's after dark, I like the heat on when you bring the car around. It takes time to warm up.'"

"But you didn't work here last year," Kerry pointed out.

Josh jabbed the glowing end of his cigarette at her to emphasize his point. "Exactly," he said. "But you think reality matters to this guy? Like I'm the first Goth valet in California history or something, so it couldn't have been someone else he told last year. He's so convinced it was me, he stiffed me on the tip."

Kerry pushed aside the hand that held the cigarette. She had made clear, plenty of times, what she thought of that habit and couldn't understand how he managed to reconcile it with his vegan lifestyle. "Hey," he had said when she'd raised the question once, "who said life was free of contradiction? Anyway it's a vegetable. If tobacco had a face, I wouldn't smoke it." Sympathetically, in spite of the noxious weed, she rubbed Josh's bony shoulder. "There are always a few pains," she said. "But most of the guests are pretty nice."

"Maybe to you," Josh countered. "You can spit in their food. All I can do is adjust their seat backs wrong, and the potential threat level just isn't the same."

Kerry laughed then and punched the shoulder she had just been rubbing. "I'll tell you what," she offered. "I'll trade places with you for a day. You deal with complaints about food being too hot or too cold or too spicy or too bland, and guys grabbing your ass and winking at you like you're going to go, 'Oh, you're just so handsome. I'll put this tray of food down and meet you in the alley.'"

"I guess it depends on the guy," Josh suggested with a smile she could see in the glow of his cigarette embers as he inhaled. "Hey, my principles are nothing if not situational. And believe me, I'm not under any illusions that you have an easy job either."

"Summer jobs aren't supposed to be easy," Kerry replied, ignoring his jokes. "They're supposed to be brutal and demeaning and ill-paying. Toughens you up for the rest of your life."

Josh nodded. "I guess you're right." He flipped his smoke to the sidewalk and crushed it out with his shoe. "So, you ready to jet? Waiting on Mace?"

"Waiting on Mace," Kerry confirmed. It had become a house motto over the summer. Mace Winston was never ready on time for anything—he was the only person she had ever known who was perpetually late *leaving* work. She was more than ready to go—her headache from that morning had never really gone away, and working in the noise of the crowded dining room had just made it worse.

Before Josh could reply, Mace came through the kitchen door. He was a dishwasher, and the hairs on his muscular forearms were plastered to his skin by the water that had leaked into his rubber gloves. Even the sleeves of his T-shirt were wet. His broad, handsome face was flushed from the hot water he'd been working in, a line of sweat sitting on his upper lip.

He tossed Kerry a lopsided grin, as if something hurt in a place too embarrassing to mention. "You've got to start encouraging those folks to eat less," he told her. "Fewer side dishes. Better for their hearts, and better for me."

"I'll see what I can do," she said with a laugh. Neither of these guys were people she'd have been likely to hang out with under other circumstances, but over the course of the summer, they'd become close friends. Whenever she was talking with them, Kerry felt an easy, pleasant sense of comfort envelop her like a warm blanket on a cold night. It almost—but not quite—overwhelmed the sense of impending disaster her dreams had left her with and the headache that accompanied them. "Now can we go home?"

The others offered consent, as if either of

them would be likely to argue in favor of staying and working awhile longer. Kerry took one last glimpse toward the water she couldn't see, breathed in a final lungful of ocean air, and headed for the parking lot with the others.

The Seaside Resort at La Jolla, to use its full name, was as soulless and impersonal as most large corporations. But it was also a corporation that recognized the fact that its business was largely seasonal, and to help it through the busy summer season, it hired a lot of temporary workers. Summer help came from all over the world—Prague, Sydney, Heidelberg, Minsk, and even the exotic climes of King of Prussia, Pennsylvania. So the resort offered, as one of its worker-friendly perks, a roommate-matching service. Kerry had signed up, filling out the requisite forms and answering a slew of questions about things she wouldn't even have talked about with the aunt and uncle she lived with. She was slotted into a house in nearby Bird Rock with five people with whom she had in common only the fact that they all worked for Seaside.

After a few weeks of initial discomfort,

though, everyone fell into a kind of casual routine. Kerry, Josh, and Mace shared the house with Scott Banner and Brandy Pearson, who had come out from Harvard as a couple, and Rebecca Levine. The couple didn't get to share a room since there were only two bedrooms in the small cottage, and nobody was willing to cram four into one room so that two could have the other. But Brandy and Scott still managed plenty of alone time in the house, and they'd both had tonight off. They had said they were going to a movie, and as Mace pulled his massive baby blue Lincoln Continental onto the narrow driveway, Kerry noticed that Scott's RAV4 was still gone.

"Guess the lovebirds are still out on the town," Josh pointed out, echoing Kerry's observation.

"Too bad for them," Mace said, without a hint of sympathy. The driveway ran alongside the house, crowded on one side by the neighboring house's oleander bushes and on the other by the cottage itself. There was room for both cars if the RAV4 got tucked in first, but when Mace's monstrosity had pulled in as far as it could, the RAV4's rear end wouldn't clear the sidewalk. Which meant he had to park on the street. Mace had urged him just to block the sidewalk a little, but Scott was full of Harvard-induced social activism and refused to in case someone came by in a wheelchair. Kerry admired the stand he took, but couldn't have said for sure if she would be as noble if she had to be the one looking for street parking late at night.

The cottage was dark, as if Brandy and Scott had left during the day and had forgotten that no one would be home until after eleven. Rebecca had been working early shifts, and was no doubt already sound asleep—the girl could sleep anywhere, through anything, Kerry had decided.

The nearest streetlight was half a block away, largely obstructed by a big willow tree that overhung most of the miniscule front yard. A low hedge ringed the front of the house, bisected by a flagstone walkway that led from the sidewalk to the front steps. Their landlord paid for landscaping. If it'd been left up to the six of them, Kerry was sure everything would have died by July.

"Somebody could've left a light on," Josh

complained, fumbling in his pocket for keys. "I can't even see the front door."

"Like they're gonna think of that," Mace replied quickly. "Probably too heavy into lip-lock mode when they walked out. And Sleeping Beauty was most likely out before the sun went down."

Having no flashlight handy, Kerry, who was not yet out of the Lincoln, hung back to hold the door open in case its dome light could cast a little illumination to help Josh. With considerable and fluent cursing, Josh managed to jam his key into the lock and got the door open. Inside, he flipped switches, and light blasted out from the coach lamp by the door, the windows, and the gaping doorway.

Light that etched, among other things, a pair of legs sticking out of the hedge. Male legs, it looked like, clad in dark pants, feet in what Kerry guessed were expensive leather ankle-high boots. She realized that a far more appropriate response to noticing the legs would have been to scream rather than, well, *noticing* them.

But the scream, practiced so often recently in dreams, wouldn't come. It caught in her throat like a chicken bone. Instead she barely rasped out Mace's name, since his back was still visible in the doorway.

"Mace . . ."

He turned, gave her a questioning look.

"Mace," she said again, a little more forcefully.

"What's up, Kerry?"

She pointed toward the hedge. Taking a step closer, she could see that the man, whoever he was, had crashed through the brush and was laying mostly covered by its greenery. "Umm . . . he doesn't belong there."

Finally Mace noticed him. "Oh, Jesus, Kerry. Get inside, I'll call the cops."

"I don't know if he needs cops," Kerry said, inching closer. "An ambulance, maybe."

"He's just some drunk, Kerry," Mace argued. "Fell down there and couldn't wake up."

But Kerry didn't think so. She'd been around enough drunks—held the hair away from friends' faces when they got sick, dodged clumsily groping hands at parties, even tucked her own uncle Marsh into bed a time or two or ten—to know the stink that wafted around them like a foul cloud. The closer she got to this man, though, the more she knew the smell was all wrong. Instead of the miasma of alcohol, there was a familiar metallic tang. The man in the hedge was very still and silent, and she moved closer still, as Mace watched, frozen, from the doorway.

The smell was blood, and it was thick in the air around the man.

Crap, she thought. *He's been stabbed. Or shot.*

She knew there was no way he hurt himself that much falling through the hedge. He'd have been scratched up—*could even have put out an eye on a branch*—but he wouldn't have opened enough veins to kick up a stench like a blood bank on two-for-one day. Kerry had nursemaided her mom for years while cancer had spread throughout her body, finally taking the older woman. Kerry was no trained doctor, but she'd learned a little something about emergency medical care during the ordeal, and she had a feeling that this guy was going to need everything she could offer and then some.

Another smell, underlying the one of blood, nagged at her, and Kerry suddenly realized that it was a faint electrical stink of ozone, as if lightning had struck close by.

"I don't think he needs the police," she repeated, leaning forward to find the man's wrist in hopes of checking his pulse. By now, she noticed, Josh's lean form had appeared in the doorway, silhouetted behind Mace. "At least not first thing. He needs a paramedic."

The hand she had been groping for clamped around her forearm with surprising strength. "No," the man said, his voice an anxious rasp almost indistinguishable from the rustling sound his motion made in the hedge. "No doctors."

Her heart jumped to her throat, and she tried to yank her arm free. But the man held fast to it, even raising his head a little to look at her. A stray beam from the streetlight shone through the leaves onto his right eye, making it gleam like something from a Poe story. "Promise me, no doctors," he insisted. "Take me in and give me shelter or leave me here, but let me live or die on my own terms."

Mace and Josh had both come down from the doorway and hovered over Kerry and the wounded man like anxious seagulls at the beach, looking for handouts. "Dude, let her go," Mace ordered, snarling. "Or I'll really put a hurtin' on you."

She heard Mace shift as if he really did intend to attack the wounded man, and then she did something that surprised even her. She spread her one free arm—the man on the ground continued to clutch her right arm with a grip so powerful she didn't think she could have shaken it—over the man, as if to protect him from whatever Mace might have in mind. "No!" she shouted. "He's hurt bad enough. Leave him alone or help me bring him inside, but don't be stupid."

"I've got to wonder about your definition of stupid," Mace said, sounding petulant.

"He's right, Kerr," Josh added. "You want to bring some bloody stranger into our house?"

"You guys both missed Sunday school the day they talked about the good Samaritan?" Kerry shot back over her shoulder. "If you don't want to help me, just get out of the way. He's losing blood and he can't stay out here overnight." She pushed her way deeper into the thick hedge, feeling the branches scratch and tear at her skin like a hundred cats' claws, snagging her long, fine black hair and the fabric of the white cotton dress shirt that, with snug black pants, was her restaurant uniform.

She reached around the stranger's head with her left hand, hoping she could ease him up out of the hedge. Holding back the worst of the branches with her own body so he wouldn't suffer any further injury, she found the back of his head and slipped her hand down to support his neck. His hair was long in back, and matted with sticky blood. Never mind the tears, the bloodstains would make her uniform shirt unwearable.

"That's crazy talk," Mace complained behind her. She ignored him and drew the man slowly forward.

Josh unleashed another string of colorful profanities, but he knelt beside Kerry and shoved branches out of the way, helping to bring the wounded man out of the hedge. "I guess we need to get the mug out of our bushes anyway."

"You're both crazy, then," Mace opined. Kerry couldn't see Mace, but from the sound of it, she gathered that he had given up on them both and was on his way back inside. She found herself hoping that it wasn't to get a baseball bat or to call 911.

What do I care? she wondered. The good

Samaritan thing had been a flip response to Mace and Josh's moaning, but it wasn't any kind of lifestyle choice she had made. She guessed that, as Josh might say, it meant the reaction she was having in this case was situational. Something about this battered, broken man in their bushes played on her sympathy, and she was unwilling to leave him there or to go against his stated wishes by calling the authorities.

With Josh's assistance she was able to disentangle the man from the hedge. In the light, the blood on his face was shocking—dark and glistening and obviously fresh. He might have been handsome once, but age and the damage caused by whatever had done this to him had taken care of that. She felt, more than ever, an urgency about getting him inside, getting his bleeding stopped, and trying to prevent shock.

"Can you stand up?" she asked him, not sure if he was even still conscious. But he forced his eyes open again, raised his head, and looked at her with something like kindness. His mouth curled into an agonized smile.

"Not a chance," he whispered. Then his head drooped, his eyes closed, his muscles went limp. For the first time, his grip on her forearm eased. She touched his neck, felt the pulse there.

"He's still alive," she declared.

"But he's deadweight," Josh said. Josh was, well . . . "lean" was a polite way to put it. "Scrawny" was more the truth. And the stranger was a big man, probably a little more than six feet tall, weighing a couple hundred pounds. "You think we can carry him?"

Kerry spoke without hesitation, without doubt. "We can carry him. You take his feet."

"Oh, I almost forgot," Josh said. He used the name that the housemates had applied to Kerry ever since they'd become familiar with her stubborn streak, "Bulldog."

Hoisting the stranger's shoulders, she grinned at Josh way down at the other end. "Woof."

Just for fun I looked back to see my first impressions of my housemates. Thinking to compare them, I guess, to current impressions.

Just goes to show how wrong you can be sometimes.

"Can you say insufferable?" I had typed about Josh Quinn. "Gay, Goth, vegan, and obnoxiously adamant about all three. If he keeps it up, I'll be surprised if he survives the summer. Not that he could be 'voted out' or whatever. Not that, to push the metaphor to the breaking point and beyond, this is a reality TV show or anything. _The Real World_, _Big Brother_, _Survivor_—they have nothing on the trials and tribs of six genuine strangers trying to get along in a house without cameras, supercool furniture, and a cash prize on the other end."

There was more, but why cut-and-paste all night when I can simply scan the folder menu and look it up? Suffice to say, his first impression was the kind that almost makes you hope it'll also be a last impression.

Mace Winston, on the other hand. Then, I wrote: "Hmm . . . he's got a body like Michelangelo's David— not that I've seen under the fig leaf, figuratively speaking. But handsome, buff, and he tooled up in this sky blue Lincoln Continental—except for the left rear, I think he said quarter-panel, which is kind of rust colored and clearly taken from a different car. He said he found the whole thing in a desert canyon somewhere in New Mexico, full of bullet holes and snakes, but he cleaned it up and fixed it up and here he is. He really does wear the boots and one of those straw hats and he has squinty, twinkly eyes like Josh Hartnett or Clint Black and somehow it all works for him. I don't know if there's a brain in his head. Ask me later if I care."

But tonight, when the chips, as they say, were down, Mace turned away and Josh came through. Although the heaving and ho-ing would have gone better had it been the other way around, I'm sure.

Okay.

Ms. Harrington, in eleventh-grade speech, used to give us holy hell when we started with "okay" or "umm." She said it was just a verbal time waster, a way of saying that our thoughts obviously weren't well enough organized to begin with because if they were, we'd start out by saying what we really wanted to say.

Boy, was she right.

So . . . okay. Umm . . .

There's a man in our living room, passed out on

that butt-sprung lump of fabric and wood that passes for a sofa. We managed to stop most of the bleeding, put bandages on the worst cuts, got a couple of blankets (mine, since no one else would volunteer theirs) over him, elevated his feet higher than his head. Near his head there's a glass of water, in case he wakes up and is thirsty, and he seems to be breathing okay.

He looks like he lost an argument with a wood chipper. I can't even imagine what happened to him. Hit by a truck that hurled him all the way across our lawn? Picked up by a stray tornado and dropped there?

But he said no doctors, and that's exactly how many he's getting. Why? And why did I argue against calling the police? Rebecca woke up just before Scott and Brandy finally came home. I had the same argument with them that I'd had with Mace, although Scott came over to my side pretty quickly and Rebecca, bless her huge hippie heart, lit a candle and dug right in to help with the bandaging. With Josh already allied, that made four against two—Mace and Brandy. Brandy did a lot of huffing noises and is now either sound asleep, or pretending to be, as I laptop this. Is that a verb yet? If not, how soon?

Other good verbs: To delay. To procrastinate. To put off.

Okay.

Of course, what I wanted to do with my summer was to lead a life that might, by some reasonable definition, be normal. As opposed to the life I've led for the past, well, lifetime. Summer job, summer friends, maybe a summer boyfriend, even. Just, y'know, normal stuff.

I don't think this qualifies.

And to be fair, they're entirely correct (and "they" know who they are). We don't know who he is—he could be dangerous, a felon, a crazy person. Or even, you know, someone from Lenny Kravitz's band, although maybe a little senior for that. But, to continue being fair, he's not the one who said "no cops." That was, not to put too fine a point on it, me. He just said "no doctors," and maybe he's a Christian Scientist or whatever. I was the one who said "no cops," and I'm still not sure why I did that. But it was the right thing to do.

I hope.

Journaling is supposed to help one figure out one's own emotions, right? Tap into the unconscious, puzzle out the mysteries therein? Not tonight, Dr. Freud. I don't know why I trust the old road-kill guy snoozing on the couch. But I do.

Go figure. Go to sleep. Go to hell. Just go. See you tomorrow, if we're not all murdered in our sleep. Or lack thereof.

More later, I hope.

K.

2

Scott Banner was one of those guys who did lots of things well. Kerry hadn't known him all that long, but then it didn't take long to figure that out about him. He got good grades in school, hence the Harvard bit. He worked hard, he could cook and clean quickly and efficiently, which were pluses where Kerry was concerned because that meant fewer household chores that she had to do around the summer house. He played soccer, and he looked fit and trim in the polo shirts, khakis, and Topsiders that he favored, and while Kerry thought he was dressing about twenty years ahead of his age, he somehow managed to pull it off.

His girlfriend Brandy, black, athletic, and as graceful as Kerry was not, appreciated those things about him too, confiding to Kerry that he would make someone a great husband one day, hoping that someone would be her. Kerry thought they made a wonderful couple, occasionally wishing she had someone who matched her as well as Scott and Brandy did each other.

One of the most important things to know about Scott was that he made really excellent coffee. And for those occasions when he wasn't available, there was a spot called Java Coast in downtown La Jolla, next to an English as a foreign language school that attracted vast numbers of young, available men—all foreign, of course, but Kerry had picked up a few words of Spanish, French, German, and Russian over the summer. The mornings that she worked early or that Scott was otherwise unavailable for barista duties, she allowed herself to splurge on the pricey brews there. All of which went to the fact that, on this particular morning, having slept almost not at all, Kerry had the distinct feeling that there just wasn't going to be enough coffee in the world to get her through the day. She had developed a serious caffeine habit over the summer. But some days it was more crucial than others.

Today she sniffed the air hopefully, even before she rolled out of the sack. No fragrant aroma of the glorious bean. So Scott was sleeping in, or Brandy had been ticked enough about the way last night's argument had gone that she had kicked him out of the house or dragged him away for an early breakfast (and accompanied by a stern talking-to).

Or, of course, it meant that the stranger in their living room had in fact been an axe murderer, and all of her housemates were dead.

With that image in her mind, she kicked off the sheets and glanced at herself. Green cotton pajama pants and a tank top provided enough coverage. She padded barefoot across the hardwood floor, pulled the door open. A short hallway led to the living room, and she could smell the man before she saw him. He was still there, and he needed a shower more than ever. But if he had, in fact, murdered the rest of the household, she'd have expected him to smell more like fresh blood—as he had last night—and less like stale sweat.

So all in all, an improvement over where things *could* have been.

And there had been no nightmares during

the night, she realized, which was a bonus. She'd had recurrent nightmares before, but not since the days when she was young enough to comfort herself by hugging the rag-doll clown she'd named BoBo. He was long since put away, though, stored in a trunk in her uncle Marsh's attic. Approaching the stranger, she found herself wishing for a moment that she had BoBo here with her, giving her courage as he had done when she was a child.

The living room was dimly lit—curtains still drawn, but they were moth-eaten and sunshine leaked through—and nobody was around. Kerry approached the stranger, whose breath was ragged but steady, and looked at his pale, drawn face. He looked different, somehow, than he had the night before. Still gaunt, but his cheeks seemed less sunken, the hollows of his eyes shallower than they had been. It was almost as if, she thought, the night's sleep had not only allowed him to heal but had made him younger at the same time.

Even so, Rolling Stones young, not Radiohead young. Big difference.

A sound from behind her. Kerry turned. Rebecca, her short-cropped orange hair reaching in every direction at once, stood there in blue fuzzy slippers and a cotton nightgown. Rebecca took a bath every day, never a shower, and she spent a minimum of forty minutes—more often an hour—in the bathroom. Lit candles, put in a bath bomb or bubble bath, something floral. Pampered herself. Kerry admired her dedication even if—in a house with six people and only one bathroom and a half—she often resented the time it took. But a cloud of flowery fragrance usually surrounded Rebecca, as it did now, wafting to Kerry's nose across the room, providing relief from the stranger's stench.

Rebecca blinked away sleep. "I stayed up last night," she said in a quiet voice. "Watching him."

Kerry felt an unexpected surge of jealousy, as if the strange man sleeping on their couch was her find, not anyone else's. She knew it made no sense. *Just tired,* she decided. She hadn't stayed up watching him. Thinking about him, though. "Did he do anything?"

A shrug. "Just slept. Maybe dreamed some—he moaned a little, and kind of scrunched his face up, you know."

"How long did you watch him?" Kerry asked, hoping the answer wasn't long enough to be creepy.

"Just awhile," Rebecca said, shrugging some more. Kerry had learned that was one of her signature moves. Maybe a sign of low self-esteem, as if to accompany her statements with a shrug meant that they shouldn't be taken too seriously. "I think he's getting better."

Kerry had to agree, though it was absurd to think that just a few hours of sleep would make much difference to a man as wounded as he'd been. *Well,* she mentally corrected, *a few hours of sleep and some basic first aid.*

But she had thought the same thing when she first glanced at him. Now, as if disturbed by their soft conversation, the man on the couch groaned and rolled away from them. She waited another few moments, thinking that he might wake up. When he didn't, she looked at Rebecca and stifled a yawn against the back of her hand. "Let's make some java, Beck," she said.

Rebecca happily agreed.

A few hours passed. The day, as they had a tendency to do in San Diego in August, heated up. Kerry put on a green V-neck T-shirt with soft, faded jeans and the red-and-white zigzag sneakers that were even more comfortable than being barefoot, and brought a book into the living room. She sat in the big easy chair that had come with the furnished house, silently turning pages while she watched over her patient. The last thing she wanted was for him to wake up alone, in a strange room, not knowing where he was or who had brought him there. She plugged a freestanding fan over by the doorway, hoping its whir wouldn't be too loud. The breeze wasn't exactly cool but at least it moved the air around.

Occasionally one of her housemates—none of whom, as it happened, had been murdered in their sleep—would wander by. When Mace came in he stood with his hands on his hips and cocked his chin toward the sleeping man. "Dude still alive?"

"Seems to be," Kerry told him. "Disappointed?"

"Surprised, I guess," Mace answered. "Didn't think he'd make it to dawn."

"I guess he's tougher than he looks," Kerry observed.

"Seems like." He shook his head and moseyed on.

When it was time for Kerry to leave for work, she called in sick. It was the first time she had done so all summer, and a pang of guilt caught in her stomach when she hung up the phone. But her boss, Mr. Hofstadter, wouldn't have understood or accepted the real reason.

Through it all, the man slept. And Kerry wondered about him.

What was his story? How had he wound up in their yard? What had injured him? Was anyone looking for him? These questions, and many more, kept her from concentrating on her book, a paperback chick-lit novel she'd borrowed from Brandy. Her own tastes tended more toward suspense and thrillers, and if there were some exotic locations and romance mixed in, so much the better. But she would read anything she got her hands on, and this one was available.

Every time the man shifted in his sleep, she tensed, thinking he was waking up. The rest of the household went to work. She paced, or sipped a soda, or tried to read, and waited.

Eventually she dozed off in the chair. The

book slid to the floor, but that didn't wake her.

Neither did having a blanket draped over her.

Later, she did open her eyes, startled that they had been closed at all. More startled to see that the man was sitting up on the couch, watching her. On her lap she clutched the blanket that had once covered him.

"You didn't have to do all this," he said. His voice was soft and smooth, not the ragged husk of the night before. His eyebrows raised as if to encompass the "all this" to which he referred.

He was definitely younger than he had looked, even that morning. Sleep and recuperation had erased wrinkles, filled furrows. Still years older than her, but maybe not decades. His eyes were steel gray and clear, dancing with a light all their own in the poorly lit room.

She patted at the blanket. "It looks kind of like you're the one who's been taking care of me."

"I owed you," he said, as if that explained everything.

Or, really, anything.

"All I did was—"

He cut her off. His smile was, she realized,

quite enchanting. "All you did was take me in, against the wishes of most of your friends. Clean and dress my wounds. Allow me to sleep, undisturbed, for as long as I needed. Accept without question my desire not to be taken to a doctor. Refuse to call the police. That, I have to say, was more than I could have asked, even if I'd been capable of asking, and I appreciate it."

Kerry blinked a couple of times. "Weren't you, like, unconscious for most of that?"

"Yes," he said, flashing her that grin again. She felt it down to her toes. She hadn't noticed what a handsome man he was—or, more accurately, how it had been obscured by the apparent years with which his pain and exhaustion had saddled him. "But not unaware. Thank you for everything."

As he spoke he made to rise from the couch, pushing off with his right hand. But he hadn't even reached his full height when his legs buckled, and he flopped back down. He tossed her a sheepish smile that dimpled his cheeks. "I guess I'm not as strong as I thought."

Kerry rushed to his side to help him, dropping the blanket to the floor. "You shouldn't even be awake, much less trying to stand," she insisted. He was already sitting by the time she reached him, so she wasn't sure what to do with herself. She stood there a few moments, feeling embarrassed, then simply sat down beside him as if that had been her plan all along.

Graciously he ignored her awkwardness and extended a hand. "My name is Daniel Blessing," he said.

She took his hand in her own. His was large, engulfing hers, and as warm as if he'd been holding a cup of hot tea. Holding it felt comfortable, like being hugged by an old friend. After a few moments she realized he was waiting for her to let go, to say her own name, or both. She couldn't understand why she was so flustered around this man.

Except maybe because he should be dead, she thought. *Or at the very least, still comatose. And years older.*

There was something very strange going on here. Part of her wanted to know what it was, but a bigger part—the dominant part, she realized—wondered why she wasn't more concerned about why she trusted him, almost instinctively. Why she had brought him into the house and dismissed the concerns of housemates who didn't want to leave her alone with him.

"Kerry," she managed at last. "I'm Kerry Profitt."

"Yes," he said, as if that name meant something to him. Though, obviously, it couldn't have. His voice and his manner were both, Kerry thought, oddly formal. "Yes, of course. It's a pleasure to meet you, Kerry."

"You too . . . Daniel," she replied. She had almost called him "Mr. Blessing," something about his age and that strange formality making her feel like she ought to treat him as she would a friend of her aunt Betty and uncle Marsh. She regarded his handsome face again: high forehead; intense, heavy-lidded gray eyes; a straight nose that she might have considered large on a different face but that here seemed somehow fitting. His lips were thin but quick to smile. When he did smile, his whole face took part, cheeks creasing, eyes crinkling, dimples at the edges of his mouth carving themselves into his skin. His jawline was pronounced but firm, his chin square. Thick brown hair, which could've used an encounter with water and shampoo, swept away from his brow, covering his ears, flowing over the collar of the Deftones T-shirt they'd borrowed from Mace when his own torn and blood-soaked shirt had to be cut from his damaged body. Impossibly he looked even closer to her age than he had when she'd suddenly awoken—within a decade of her, she guessed now, or not much more.

"You have questions," he said. He tried to stand again, stopped mid-rise to wince and grasp at his ribs where his worst injury had been, an open gash that looked like he'd been attacked with a meat cleaver. His skin blanched, eyes compressing against the evident pain. But he composed himself and pushed through it.

"Well, yeah, Sherlock."

"I wish I could answer them for you, Kerry. Really, I do. But if I did—well, you saw what I looked like when you brought me in, right?"

She had hardly stopped remembering. His body was lean, with the stringy musculature of someone who worked hard rather than worked out, and yardstick-wide shoulders and a deep chest—but after last night, bruised and shredded, as if he'd made a dozen laps in a demolition derby, only without a car. "Yeah, I saw."

He nodded gravely. "If I answered your questions, then you'd be at risk for the same. And, I suspect, you'd have a harder time surviving it than I did."

"So this is, what, a regular thing for you?" she asked, surprised at his use of the present tense.

He showed that grin again. "Not to this extent, no. And I don't know if I'd use the word 'regular.' But it has happened before and likely will again. I'd rather you didn't get mixed up in it, so that's all I'll say about that." He walked away from the couch, away from her—stiff-legged, clearly sore, but still, considering the shape he had been in, miraculous. "If you don't mind," he called over his shoulder, "I'm starving. Okay if I raid the kitchen?"

He's gone.

I can't quite sort out how I feel about it. Night before last I risked the wrath of my homies—and maybe our lives—playing Florence Nightingale to a stranger who could have been just what Mace and Brandy were sure he was—a random drunk who'd been bounced off somebody's fender. But once he woke up, once the years fell away from him and he started to speak, it didn't take long to see that he was not that. Still, mega-mystery man.

But we talked and eventually the others came home from work—where, they lied, I had been sorely missed—and Daniel Blessing seemed to draw energy from them. He became enchanting: witty, interesting, the kind of conversationalist to whom you could apply the term "sparkling" without being too off base. Even those who had distrusted him the most had been charmed.

Did he tell us anything about himself other than his name? He did not. And that name is probably as fake as the phone number Rebecca gives out to the tourists who hit on her at work (aside, in case I didn't mention it: While Rebecca considers herself a few pounds overweight, what she is is zaftig. She hides it with the hunching and the baggies, but the powers at Seaside picked her—being the only one of us over twenty-one—to be a cocktail waitress in their oh-so-cleverly named bar, the Schooner. Part of the cocktail waitressing involves wearing a uniform that, while not as desperately provocative as they probably were ten or twenty years ago, is still, let's just say . . . snug. And short-ish. So the aforementioned hitting on? Happens a lot).

So no personal details from (possibly) Mr. Blessing. But he was informed and erudite, able to discuss books and movies and modern music, as well as the state of the world (about which he's not much impressed), environmental and social issues, and even, much to Josh's amazement, film noir of the thirties and forties. By the time people dragged themselves away from the kitchen table to go to bed, he had won them all over. I'm only guessing, but I think Josh may have fallen a little bit in love.

He may not even have been alone in that.

But then, this morning. Not just early-ish, but genuinely early. The kind of early where your eyelids are sort of glued together and the clock's face swims just out of focus. He taps on my door a couple of times, then lets himself in before I can mumble incoherently. He kneels—*kneels!*—beside the bed, takes my hand, kisses it once, says, "Thank you, Kerry Profitt. Thank you so much, for all you've done," and then he stands up and walks out.

I fumbled out of bed, but I heard the front door close before I reached the entrance to my room, and when I hit the street, he was gone. Out of sight. Maybe there was a car waiting for him, though I didn't see or hear one. Maybe one of those big mythological birds picked him up. Or a UFO.

Gone.

I only knew him for a day. And *knew* may be too strong a word, since I know so little about him even now.

So why does it feel like there's a vast emptiness in the house?

Anyone?

3

"I'm worried about Kerry," Brandy confided. She and Scott were both at work—she as a front-desk clerk at the resort, and Scott as a groundskeeper. A couple of times a shift, they made a point of crossing paths, usually when she was on a short break from the desk. With the run of the property, his schedule was less restrictive than hers. And as a groundskeeper whose clothing could frequently be grass-stained or otherwise soiled, him visiting her at the desk was frowned upon. Now they wandered the paved pathways that led from the room complexes down to the tennis courts and pool and the wide sandy beach beyond.

"Why?" Scott wondered. He carried a broom and a long-handled dustpan in his left fist; the fingers of his right hand were twined with Brandy's darker ones.

"It's been, what, four days since that guy left. Daniel?"

"Yeah, I guess so," Scott agreed, not quite getting what she was leading to. But that was the thing about Brandy—directness was not her strong point. She would walk all the way around an issue before she'd step right up to it. "What about it?"

"She's been kind of, I don't know, mopey. Ever since."

"Brandy, she hardly knew the guy. She wanted to play nursemaid, she did, he got better. End of story."

Her grasp tightened on his fingers, and he saw the fire flash in her eyes that always told him when he'd said the wrong thing. It was not an unfamiliar event, but it was never a pleasant one either.

"It *should* be," she insisted. "But it's not, and that's the problem. Haven't you seen her? I don't know if she's laughed once since he left. This is Kerry we're talking about. Girl loves to laugh. But instead she's been acting like her dog died."

Scott knew he was treading dangerous ground. Brandy, a psych major, was perfectly content to psychoanalyze anyone who fell onto her radar screen. Scott preferred life a little closer to the surface of things, where motives and rationales were not examined so closely. And he admired Kerry's surface a great deal. She was absolutely gorgeous—he'd thought that the moment he'd met her, and hadn't stopped since. Long, silken hair of purest jet, big emerald eyes, a lean body that was not as athletic as Brandy's or as curvaceous as Rebecca's, but still feminine and attractive. He'd been with Brandy for three years, and loved her completely. But that didn't mean he didn't think once in a while about what it would be like to be with Kerry, who was almost Brandy's exact opposite, physically.

"You're right, I guess," he ventured, shaking off the mental image of Kerry to focus on Brandy. "Maybe seeing him on the couch like that, taking care of him, reminded her of her mom. When she had to take care of her for so long."

Brandy nodded. He'd scored one. "There you go, Scotty," she said, her tone congratulatory.

She stopped, released his hand and faced him, moving into lecture mode. Behind her, the Pacific surged up onto the beach, then slipped back into itself in an unending, slightly irregular rhythm. "What defined Kerry for years? Being her mom's nurse and caretaker. Then what happened to her? Her mom died anyway, and she had to move in with an aunt and uncle she can barely stand. Now she's got a nice insurance settlement, but she's working anyway, trying to supplement the money with income from a summer job. She's looking to redefine herself in some other role, but when that guy fell into her lap, almost literally, it took her back to the same place she had been, emotionally, with her mom. And when he left too . . . well, that brought back a lot of feelings, most of them the bad kind."

"Do you have a suggestion?" Scott asked. He readily admitted that he was nuts about Brandy. She was smart and beautiful and very caring, so what was not to like? But when she got like this, sometimes he felt antsy, eggshell-walking.

The first time he'd introduced her to his brother Steve—six years older, married with a kid of his own—Steve had taken him aside and said in a conspiratorial tone, "She's great, Scott. Doesn't seem like someone who puts up with idiots."

"She doesn't," Scott had confirmed.

"Then I have one piece of advice, bro. Don't be an idiot."

Brandy's little brother DJ had been less subtle. "You ever hurt my sister," he said with a sinister smile, "I won't have to do jack. That girl'll have you for breakfast and pick her teeth with your bones."

All things considered, eggshells didn't seem so bad.

"She's got to work through it her own way," Brandy prescribed, drawing Scott back to the current situation. "All we can do is be as supportive as we can, let her talk it out if she wants. Show her we care about her, but not that we want to meddle."

If amateur psychiatry wasn't meddling, Scott wasn't sure what was. But he kept that opinion to himself. Anyway, there was a stretch of lawn that needed mowing, and Brandy's break was over as was his own. He agreed with her, kissed her good-bye, and went back to work.

• • •

With so many new faces to look at every day, Kerry found herself looking forward to getting acquainted with the resort's regulars—those who stayed for a week or so and ate in the restaurant several times instead of availing themselves of La Jolla's many other fine dining opportunities. Some she got to know, on the most superficial of levels, as people on vacation who sometimes had a tendency to talk about their lives—family members, pets they left behind, the old neighborhood back in Lincoln or Tempe or Fort Wayne. Others kept their own confidences, and sometimes Kerry entertained herself by making up her own stories about them, giving them colorful, mysterious histories and reasons for visiting southern California.

Some of these fictions she had e-mailed to her best friend Jessica Tait, who had moved to Florida the year before. Lately Jessica had seemed more and more distant, as if her new life and friends were drawing her away from the bond they'd shared. Kerry mourned the change; losing her mother had been bad enough, losing her best friend on top of it was heartwrenching. The way she'd grown up had left her with precious few friends anyway, and she valued the ones she had.

Tonight one of the diners in her section was a woman she'd seen several times recently—not for days in a row, as was typical with vacationers who came to the resort, but spread out over many weeks. This was unusual, but not unheard of. Sometimes local residents decided they liked the kitchen's offerings. Carolyn Massey, the chef, had, after all, trained at Le Cordon Bleu in France, and then had a stint under Alice Waters in her Berkeley restaurant, Chez Panisse, before taking over the resort's kitchen. Her meals were always delicious and frequently adventurous.

This guest, though, Kerry noticed partly because the woman always dined alone, and partly because, while she was unfailingly pleasant and polite, there was an air about her that made Kerry believe that she was terribly sad. She was a beautiful woman, with skin so soft and smooth it could have been freshly poured from a bottle, and hair that reminded Kerry of a ray of golden afternoon sunlight shining down on fresh straw. Upon closer inspection, the color of her shoulder-blade-length hair spanned a spectrum, from platinum white to a dark auburn, and the overall effect was lovely. Her features could have belonged to fairy tale royalty, or to the Hollywood kind: wide-set, sparkling blue eyes, a refined yet expressive brow, a nose that was petite but was not so small it was an afterthought. Her lips were full and finely sculpted, and the determined set of her jaw implied that she was no pushover.

In Kerry's mind, the woman was a widow whose wealthy husband had died tragically young. She had tried to put his death behind her, to carry on with her life, but everywhere she went, simple things reminded her of the joy they had felt in their few years together. A song on the radio, a particular vintage of wine, even the cries of gulls on the beach, could bring an unexpected tear to her eye. Nonetheless, she made herself go out, eat in restaurants, drink that wine, listen to the radio, walk on the beach at sunset, intent on enjoying her heartbreaking memories as if he were still there beside her.

Sometimes Kerry added an extra twist to the woman's tale. She was a spy, and her husband had been killed in the line of duty. Or she was an international jewel thief, and he wasn't dead at all but simply doing a long stretch in a prison in Monaco or Majorca. She came to La Jolla because she wasn't wanted for anything in California—yet.

The woman's beauty was ageless, which inspired Kerry to even greater flights of fancy. She could have been in her midtwenties, her late forties, or any place in between. Her outfit was just as timeless—a loose-fitting white silk top that suggested rather than revealed her figure, a tan jacket, also silk, and matching pants with half-inch heels, no doubt some Italian brand that Kerry could pronounce no better than she could afford. There were hints of lines at the edges of her eyes and mouth that would, with the years, deepen and most likely make her even more lovely. She would carry her years and experiences well, Kerry believed.

After dinner the woman lingered over a cup of coffee. She exchanged pleasantries from time to time, but whenever Kerry tried to engage her in conversation, she expertly steered away from any personal topics. *Just adds to her mystery,* Kerry thought with some satisfaction.

When she went into the kitchen to pick up an order for the next table over, a party of five who had come in late after what looked like a scorching day on the beach—lobster-red foreheads, shoulders, and arms that would be painful and peeling before long—the last person she expected to see was Daniel Blessing.

But there he was, hovering near the open back door like an unwanted houseguest who wouldn't quite leave. When he saw Kerry, his lips parted in a sudden smile. This time, she noted, it didn't engage his eyes. She smiled back and arched a quizzical eyebrow his way.

"Daniel?" she said, surprised. "What are you doing here?" The cooks, bus staff, and dishwashers all ignored him, as if by prior arrangement. But Kerry had been out in the dining room for several minutes, and he could have had time to slip each one a twenty for all she knew.

He came toward her, unmistakable urgency in his step, and took her by the arm. His grip was so firm it hurt. She tried to pull away, but he held on. "Kerry," he whispered. "I hoped that you'd be safe, that helping me wouldn't put you in danger. I was wrong. You've got to leave here, right now."

Kerry laughed, but it sounded forced even to her. "In case you hadn't noticed, I'm kind of working here, Daniel."

"You're in terrible danger, Kerry. I'm not joking. Or exaggerating. You have to trust me."

That, in spite of herself, she had always done, even that very first night. And she certainly couldn't imagine any reason he might have had for trying to play a trick on her now. Unless this whole thing was one of those ridiculous TV stunts, set up to ridicule her in front of millions, he seemed absolutely serious.

"What's going on, Daniel? I can't just walk out of here."

"You have to," he insisted. He blew out a frustrated breath. "There's a woman out there, sitting by herself at a table."

"The blonde one?"

"That's her."

"She's a regular. She's perfectly harmless."

"You're wrong," he said with finality. "Remember how I was the night you found me?"

How could I forget? she wondered. *Three quarters dead, like an animal by the side of a busy highway.* "Of course."

"She's the one who did that to me. She's still after me. And now she's connected me to you." His voice had gotten louder as he tried to convince her, and Kerry noticed that some of the kitchen staff was now paying attention to them. She had to calm this guy down, fast, or she'd be out of a job.

"Look, Daniel," she whispered, "I don't really know you or anything, you know. I'm glad you're better and all, but I kind of need this job, and—"

He squeezed her arm even harder than he had before. "Kerry," he said. She found her gaze drawn to his eyes, such a strange color of gray, but steady and profoundly persuasive. "There's no time for this. She'll be—"

The kitchen door swung open and the woman was there. Now the staff did react. Carolyn Massey, the head chef, came forward with a knife in her hand. She'd been using it to chop fresh vegetables, and she didn't hold it threateningly, but it was still a big, sharp object. "I'm sorry," Carolyn said, "but this kitchen is off limits to everyone except staff." She glanced meaningfully at Kerry and Daniel. "Everyone."

The blonde woman barely spared her a

glance, but focused her attention on Daniel and on Kerry, who stood between them. "I thought you were near by," she said. Her voice was ice.

Then, she spoke another word, or maybe two. Kerry couldn't make them out, couldn't even tell what language they were in. As she spoke, she gestured toward Daniel with her right hand, a kind of swooping curlicue of a motion that seemed to encompass much of the kitchen before settling on him.

Daniel was already in motion when the big gas oven's door flipped open, seemingly of its own accord. He shoved Kerry to the side and spoke some equally strange words of his own, making a different sort of two-handed gesture. Kerry couldn't quite process what happened—it was all too fast, and way, way too weird—but it seemed that, in response to the woman's combined words and movement, the oven door had opened itself and a huge gout of flame jetted out toward Daniel, dragon's-breathlike. She felt the blast of heat suck the air from her lungs. But then it seemed that in response to whatever Daniel had done, the flame stopped in midair, as if striking an invisible shield, and turned back toward the woman.

The questions this raised were, of course, innumerable. But she didn't have a chance to ask so much as "What the hell?" before Daniel tugged her out the back door. He kept a tight grip on her arm as he ran for the parking lot, and she had to sprint to keep from falling down and being dragged along behind.

He was silent as he ran, and she had the impression that he was concentrating, intent on something she couldn't even sense. She guessed the woman was probably following them, but if she'd turned to look she'd have fallen for sure. So she let herself be led to a dark, low-slung sports car parked close to the restaurant. The doors sprung open before they reached it, and Daniel pushed her into the leather passenger seat. He ran around to the driver's side, and she could have sworn— though by this point, the evidence of her own senses was clearly not to be trusted—that the engine turned over before he was even sitting down. Slamming his door, he threw the car into reverse and backed from the parking space, then he shifted gears and the little car darted toward the exit.

Finally risking a glance behind them, Kerry saw that the blonde woman had indeed followed. She had just gotten into a car of her own, and before Daniel's vehicle had even cleared the first block, she was racing after them.

4

Daniel hung a sharp left turn on Avenida de la Playa, the car's rear end fishtailing through the intersection as they entered the main drag of the La Jolla Shores neighborhood. From outdoor cafés and restaurants, patrons stared as the screech of skidding tires battled the growl of the engine for supremacy. This time of night, there wasn't much vehicular traffic on the street, so Daniel floored the accelerator and the car burst forward like an animal released from a cage.

At La Jolla Shores Drive, he made a screaming right. This street, which connected with Torrey Pines and the "village" section of the resort town, was busier. Kerry gripped the edges of her bucket seat as Daniel swerved around cars and a city bus, then pulled back into a proper lane and rocketed through the major intersection at Torrey Pines. Kerry barely had time to notice that he had gone through a red light—the blare of horns from cars and trucks were lost behind them.

On the other side of Torrey Pines, the road was narrow and wound up the side of Mount Soledad, the hill that loomed over the town, providing a scenic backdrop and multimillion dollar views from its many estates. As they started the climb, Kerry heard another blurting of horns, which she figured was probably caused by the blonde woman pulling the same stunt Daniel had.

Daniel cursed under his breath.

"She's still behind us, isn't she?" Kerry asked. The run had shaken her fine hair free from the ponytail she wore for work, and she tried to re-gather it, but her hands were shaking as much as her voice.

"Sounds like it. I'd be surprised if she wasn't."

"So when are you going to tell me what this is all about?" Kerry demanded, trying to sound more forceful than she felt. "And what that little display in the kitchen was?"

"Another time," Daniel said. His teeth were clenched in concentration. "Hard enough getting to know this car so I can squeeze every last drop of juice out of her."

Getting to know? Kerry thought. A horrible notion struck her. "Isn't this your car?"

"I don't actually *own* a car," Daniel admitted.

"And this isn't a rental?"

He didn't answer. But then, he didn't need to. It was clear now that he'd stolen the car. *And,* she realized, *effectively kidnapped me.*

"I think you should let me out here," she suggested. "I'll walk back to work."

"You really don't want me to do that."

"I really do."

Daniel risked a glance at her even as he muscled the car around a hairpin turn. The floodlit walls and thickly hedged iron fences that separated La Jolla's wealthy from the rest of the world rushed past in a blur. "Kerry, I'll explain everything, I promise. But right now I'm trying to not get us killed, and I'm trying to leave Season behind. Which is another form, need I add, of not getting us killed. If I dropped you off, not only would she slaughter you, but it would slow me down enough to let her catch me. And I have to tell you, I'm not ready to go through that again."

He sounded convincing, or at least convin*ced,* and Kerry discovered that once again, she trusted him without knowing why. She stopped arguing and let him drive. A moment later they spotted an electric gate sliding shut behind a Mercedes that had just pulled into a driveway. "Hold on," Daniel muttered. He stomped on the brake and cranked the steering wheel at the same time. The little car shuddered and turned in an almost ninety-degree angle, and then he shot through the gate just before it closed. On the other side of the gate, he pulled off the driveway so that a high wall hid the car from the street. As he came to a stop and killed the engine, he said another word in whatever unfamiliar tongue he had used at the restaurant, and waggled his hand.

The air around the car seemed to shimmer, as if enveloped by the most severe heat waves this side of the Sahara. Through the weird haze, Kerry saw a silver-haired man and woman emerge from the Mercedes and stare in their direction. "Keep quiet," Daniel warned her in a whisper. "They can't see us, but they can hear us."

"What do you mean, they can't see us?" Kerry wanted to know, echoing his hushed tones.

"Invisibility spell," Daniel replied, tight-lipped. She could see beads of sweat forming at his brow and dripping down his temples as if from intense effort. Outside, the man and woman looked at each other in confusion, and the man shrugged. They turned away and went up to the door of the house, then disappeared inside. A moment later the exterior lights went dark.

Daniel faced Kerry, a finger across his lips in the universal sign for "keep quiet." She did. There would be plenty to say later. For now, though, she would let him call the shots. He was clearly playing with forces way beyond her understanding or control. That fact stirred her to unexpected anger—she'd been swept into a game to which she didn't know the rules; hadn't known, a half hour ago, even existed. She hadn't asked to be included. And yet here she was. She fumed, but silently.

But when he says I can talk again . . .

From the other side of the wall, they heard the growl of a powerful engine, and headlights swept past, shining through the iron gates. Kerry and Daniel sat in silence until the engine noise faded away, moving higher up the hill. A few moments later Daniel started the stolen car again. With a word and a wave at the gate, it slid open and Daniel drove back out onto the street.

Instead of turning right to continue toward the top of Mount Soledad, he made a left, back down the hill toward where they'd started.

"Are you taking me back to work?" Kerry asked.

"I can't do that," he said. "You're not safe there anymore. She knows she can find you there."

There was so much that Kerry didn't understand. "But she wasn't after me," she insisted. "She was after you."

"She'll consider you an ally of mine now. She's ruthless, Kerry. If I took you back there, the rest of your life would be measured in hours, maybe days at the most. I'm sorry, but you can't go back to work, and you can't go back home—she has probably located the house by now. I'm almost sure of it, in fact. How else could she have traced you to the restaurant? I never visited you there, so she must have followed you from home."

"I told you, she eats there all the time," Kerry said. She was still upset, still ticked that this guy had come along and upended her life, yanked her into his own personal drama.

If it hadn't been for what she had seen the woman do in the kitchen, she'd think Daniel suffered from paranoid hallucinations. But she *had* seen it. That overruled her rage and earned him the benefit of the doubt, at least for a while.

Daniel seemed to puzzle over what Kerry had pointed out for a few moments as he drove to the bottom of the hill and hung a right on La Jolla Parkway, heading away from town. "I didn't think that precognition was one of her gifts," he said. "But I suppose it's possible. Maybe she was staking you out, knowing that you and I would somehow come into contact."

The talk of precognition and gifts made Kerry's blood run cold. It sounded like something out of one of those movies full of pounding death metal, where everyone in the audience dresses in black and none of them could pass through an airport scanner without setting off sirens. She shivered and hugged herself, but at the same time felt a sudden weariness, as if all her strength had left her at once. Since the woman had walked into the kitchen, Kerry had been frightened and furious in more or less equal measures. Then the chase, the invisibility, the escape . . . she realized that adrenaline had been charging through her system, and now that the immediate threat had passed, it drained from her. She remained scared—probably more so than before, a combination of fear that she was in the company of a crazy man, and worse, what it might mean if he were not crazy at all—and angry that she had somehow been punished for what she had believed was a simple good deed. *See if I ever help a half-dead man in my bushes again. It's just not worth it.*

"You're going to have to do some explaining, Daniel," she declared. "And it better be good."

"It will be," he assured her with a hint of a smile. That smile, on another occasion, might have won him points, but not now. Now it implied that things were less awful than they were, and Kerry wasn't sure that was possible.

"Let's just get some place safe and comfortable. I'll tell you everything. I owe you that much."

"Got that right." Another horrible thought crossed her mind. "If the house isn't safe, what about the others? My friends?"

"They've got to get out too," Daniel replied. "As quickly as possible. Are they at the house now?"

"Some of them, maybe." Kerry knew Rebecca and Josh were at Seaside. Mace had the day off, though, and Scott and Brandy had worked earlier in the day. She almost reached for her cell phone, but then remembered that her purse was still in her locker at the resort. Cell phone, ID, money, keys . . . everything she needed with her on a daily basis was gone, unless she could somehow get back to work.

And of course, by leaving the way she had, she was pretty sure there would be no job left, even if she could get back. Which meant no further income. She had put aside a little bit over the summer, depositing it via ATM to her account back in Illinois. But her ATM card, naturally, was in her purse.

All in all, this pretty much sucked.

"You've got to warn them," he said. "Get them away from there."

"What am I supposed to tell them? I'm in the dark here, remember?"

"We'll find a safe place," he promised. "When we do, just tell them to meet us there—without telling anyone else where they're going. I know it sounds melodramatic, but their lives really are in danger now."

He took one hand off the steering wheel and squeezed her left shoulder. "Kerry, I truly am sorry you got involved in this. If I could undo it, I would."

Kerry shrugged, and he took his hand away. "Yeah, well, that makes two of us."

5

The apartment Daniel rented—one he found when cruising, stopping after sighting a sign in the window of a building, going inside, paying with enough cash that the landlord was willing to dispense with the paperwork—was on the second floor of a two-story, fake-stucco monstrosity with a red tile roof and an empty pool except for a few inches of scum-filmed rainwater. It had three bedrooms, a long, narrow living room with high ceilings and a skylight, one bathroom, and a kitchen in which two people couldn't pass each other without turning sideways and inhaling. The carpet was microthin, bunched up in spots and separating at the seams in others. Josh, when he saw it, said something about it gloriously representing southern

California's "seamy underbelly," but to Kerry it was just a dump.

It was two blocks off Palm Avenue, the main drag of Imperial Beach, a community ten miles south of downtown San Diego, which was about that far south of La Jolla. At the corners on Palm were a fast-food restaurant and a gas station with a minimart, but down the side streets there were only small cottages and low-rent apartment buildings. TVs and music—salsa, hip-hop, classic rock, and Top 40 pop—could be heard from open windows most hours of the day, and night, as it turned out, competing with the constant drone of air conditioners.

It was, Kerry knew, a place she'd be very unlikely to find for herself, which made it perfect for their purposes. The electricity hadn't been turned off yet, and the landlord had agreed to let it stay on under his name for a while in exchange for yet another handful of cash. There was no phone, but Daniel had a cell so she used it to call the summer house, then Seaside. After a couple of tries, she reached everyone and convinced them to leave work or the house and to join her in Imperial

Beach. She pleaded, cajoled, and threatened, but they all came. Scott and Brandy brought her laptop and some clothes from the house, in addition to their own things and everyone else's. She gave Rebecca her combination so her friend could get her purse and personal items from work. Within four hours of her escape, as she had come to think of it, from the resort's kitchen, they were all seated together on the floor of the apartment's living room, backs against the walls, legs crossed. Daniel cleared his throat. He was on stage, and, Kerry believed, he knew it. *Looks like you got some 'splainin' to do, Lucy,* she thought, à la Ricky Ricardo.

He started by flashing his friendly grin, but Kerry was having none of that. "I know what I'm about to tell you will sound ridiculous to you," he began. "Unbelievable, even. But I swear to you, it's true. I could make you believe it—that's not a terribly difficult stunt, for me—but I won't do that. Instead I want you to believe it on its own merits. Such as they are."

Kerry, having already experienced some of his "stunts," was thrown by his passing remark about being able to make them believe. She interrupted before he could continue. "Daniel, when we first met you," she said, "and I found myself trusting you, for no particular reason . . . was that just because I really trusted you? Or did I have . . . I don't know, *help*?"

"And by 'help,' you mean . . . ?"

"You tell me."

"Was I enchanting you?" he asked. "Even through my pain and semiconsciousness?" He smiled again, looking at the others, instead of Kerry. "Yes, I was. I apologize now, but I couldn't take a chance that you'd send me to a hospital, or call the police. I had barely escaped from Season with my life, and she knew that. She'd have been watching for me to show up at a hospital. I needed a place to hide out, to recuperate, and you guys gave me that. I don't know if I thanked you enough for that, for giving me a chance to live."

Rebecca cleared her throat. "Season? Who's that?"

"Is that who we saw at the restaurant?" Kerry asked. "The one who chased us, and—"

"They're still talking about that all over the resort," Rebecca broke in. "You guys are, like, famous. Or infamous, I guess."

Daniel was nodding. "That was her. Season Howe is her name. She's a witch."

Josh made a snorting noise. "Do we get the Ouija board out now?" he asked. "Commune with the spirits of the dead? I think Rebecca has a Stephen King novel we could use for reference."

"It's not as easy as all that," Daniel said matter-of-factly. "It can be done, but according to their rules, not ours."

"Come *on*!" Scott said angrily. His features were long and narrow, their length accentuated by the large lenses on his wire-rimmed glasses and his gaunt cheeks reddened with emotion. "What kind of game are you playing here, Daniel? Why don't you get to the point and tell us what this nonsense is all about?"

"I understand your feelings," Daniel replied, staying calm. "I *am* telling you what it's about. It's about Season Howe. It always has been."

"Maybe you need to give us a little more detail," Brandy suggested. "And the kind we can believe would be good."

"But if he can enchant us," Rebecca tossed out, "how do we know *what* we can believe?

We might believe him only to find out that he *made* us believe him!"

"Which, if he could do that," Mace observed quietly, "would mean that he really is able to do this magic stuff he's claimin' to do."

"If I could go on," Daniel said, "without enchanting you or somehow causing you to believe a word that I say, except perhaps by convincing you—"

"That'd be good," Kerry said. "Because our lives? Pretty much uprooted now, thanks to you. It'd be nice if there's a good reason for it all."

"There is," he assured her. He met her gaze for a moment, solidly, and she felt once again the trust she had before. Of course, now it was tempered by the knowledge that he had helped that trust along a good bit, or at least he claimed he had.

"You have seen, Kerry, things tonight that you would never have believed a few days ago, true?"

She blinked a couple of times. "I . . . I *think* I have."

"Trust yourself, if not me," he suggested. "Trust your own senses."

"Well, then . . . yes. I saw what looked like some kind of . . . mystical battle between you and that woman—"

"Season."

"Yeah, her. Season. In the kitchen. Then we ran, and you stole a car—only without a key, or taking any time to hotwire it, or whatever. Then later on you turned it . . . invisible. So yeah, I guess it's safe to say I've seen some strange things tonight."

"The merest glimpse into my life," Daniel said, his voice grave. "Our lives. Season's . . . and mine."

"What is she, some kind of psycho ex-girlfriend?" Mace asked.

Daniel chuckled. "Hardly. An enemy. Always an enemy."

"So you've known her for a long time?" Josh wondered.

"Too long," Daniel said. His gaze had gone distant, as if he were searching his memory for something he couldn't find. "You'll find this hard to believe, I'm sure. In *spite* of the evidence you've seen tonight, Kerry. It all happened so long ago."

"How long?" Kerry asked.

Daniel cleared his throat and met her gaze again, as if only by looking into her eyes could he persuade her of the most outlandish things. "During the spring of 1704, in a town called Slocumb, Virginia—you can still find it on the map, a good map, anyway—Season was accused of witchcraft. There was plenty of evidence against her. She was, after all, a very powerful witch, and she remains one today."

Mace let out a snickering sound, and Daniel fixed him with a heated stare. "I said you'd have a hard time believing me," he reminded them. "But let me finish, please, then question me all you like."

Mace shrugged, and Daniel continued. "Season was guilty, there was no doubt of that. The town's fathers weren't hasty about this accusation. Nonetheless, Season objected to it. She objected with fire and wind and destruction. Her powers were greater than anyone in Slocumb suspected, and when her assault was over, so was the town. There was only one survivor."

"You're kidding," Kerry said, as surprised by the unexpected brutality of the story as by its outlandishness.

Daniel shook his head. "Not at all," he said. "Some of this you can find corroborated in history books. Except they don't know, or don't tell, the real reason the town was destroyed."

"Who was the survivor?" Brandy asked.

"I suppose if you look at it another way, there were three survivors," Daniel said quietly. "Since my mother was pregnant at the time with twins."

"Your mother?" Brandy was the one who spoke up, but it was obvious from the general response that they all had a hard time with this sudden twist in the tale.

"That's right," Daniel said. "Everyone called her Mother Blessing. She was also a witch, but she used her abilities to help the people of Slocumb, and she was not only accepted there, but loved. When Season's rage came, though, Mother Blessing was only able to protect herself . . . and her unborn sons—myself and my twin brother, Abraham. We were born seven months later."

"So you're sayin' you're, like, three hundred years old," Mace stated.

"Close to it," Daniel confirmed.

"No offense, bud, but the femme fatale plot is way old hat," Josh said, looking disgruntled. "And no way I buy the old man bit."

Brandy stood up, shaking her head, face clouded with anger. "Okay, now I know you're yanking our chains. I don't know why or what your scam is, but I don't appreciate you trying to play me and my friends!"

Daniel was silent while she remonstrated him, and when she was finished he spread his hands placatingly. "I told you that you'd have a hard time believing me," he reminded her. "I also said that it might be easier for Kerry, who had already seen things tonight that she would never have believed possible."

Brandy turned to Kerry. "Okay, then, Kerry," she said. "Take a look. Do you believe he's a day over a hundred? Or forty, for that matter?"

Kerry swallowed hard. She wasn't sure what she believed anymore. She wouldn't have believed he could make a car invisible, but he seemed to have done just that. And she had seen how old he had looked when they'd first brought him inside—maybe not three hundred, but certainly far older than he had even a day later.

"I . . . don't know," she admitted. "Given what I have seen, though, I'm willing to give Daniel the benefit of the doubt. At least for now."

"Until what?" Brandy pressed. "Until he makes some even more ridiculous claim? How far out there do you want him to go?"

"What will it take to convince you, Brandy?" he asked, remaining utterly calm in the face of her barrage.

"I don't know," she said. "You keep talking about Kerry, what she's seen. What about the rest of us? Why don't you show us something?"

"I don't use my abilities casually," Daniel explained. "They're not for show-and-tell—"

"Lame excuse," Brandy snapped, pointing at him.

"—but if it will help to convince you," Daniel continued, "then I'll try. Nothing fancy—I'm still getting my strength back after Season's sneak attack the other day."

"Is that how you ended up at our place?" Rebecca asked. "A sneak attack?"

"She took me by surprise, yes. I was unprepared, and she very nearly finished me right then." He closed his eyes, as if to end the conversation, and it worked. The room was almost silent. Kerry heard the breathing of her friends, her pulse pounding in her own head, and that was all.

Then Daniel's eyes snapped open and he turned to glare at Brandy, gesturing toward her with both hands and speaking a soft phrase Kerry couldn't make out. Brandy's pose remained the same—arms clenched tightly across her chest, chin jutting defiantly, legs spread a little—but her location changed. Now, instead of a couple of feet of empty space above her head, the space was beneath her feet. Her head brushed the ceiling. When she realized this, fury danced in her eyes. "Put me down!"

Daniel obliged, and a moment later Brandy was standing once again on the floor, and the others gaped at her, openmouthed. "What the hell was that?" she demanded.

"A demonstration."

"Mass hypnosis, more like," she insisted.

"Touch your hair, Brandy," Kerry urged. Brandy glared at her for a moment, but then put a hand to her head. It came away dusted with the debris her head had scraped off the popcorn-style ceiling. "That's not hypnosis."

Brandy rolled some of the plaster dust between her fingers, examining it as if the truth lay inside. In a way, Kerry figured, it did. Daniel's demonstration didn't make the rest of his absurd story true, but it at least showed that there was more to him than was readily apparent.

More to the world, for that matter.

So after that my friends, being who they are, couldn't shut up long enough for Daniel to finish telling his story. Which, I don't know about them, but I'd have liked to have heard more of.

I mean, sure, he told bits of it. His mother dedicated her life to hunting down Season Howe, bringing her to some kind of witchy justice for what she did to their town. And when her sons were grown, she dedicated them to the task too. Season, he explained, has been in hiding ever since. She goes where people are—resort towns in season, like La Jolla, are a favorite because the population temporarily swells and it's easy to stay anonymous. She'll go to one for a few years, then move so people don't get to know her too well. Once everyone she's encountered has moved on or died off, then she can start going there again.

Having figured out her pattern, Daniel said, he has been able to get close a few times. But as powerful as he is, she is more so, and she's always managed to avoid or defeat him—or, like this time, turn the tables so that the hunter is the hunted.

But the others were all over him with questions. Stupid ones too—did he know Humphrey Bogart, Josh wanted to know. Answer, no, in case anybody cares. Not that anybody's reading this except me. Brandy got completely corny and wanted to know if he'd ever lived on Elm Street, in reference to nightmares, I guess. Which is my department, after all, although not so much lately, blessed be (as they say, or do they, in witchy circles?). Did he fight in the Revolutionary War (Civil War, World Wars I and II)? I think Mace asked him about every war except the Spanish-American. Answers, no, no, no, and no. His war is private, and all-consuming.

War sucks, and his seems to be no exception. To look at him you wouldn't think he had paid too high a price. I mean, he's an older man—way older, if you believe him (do I? "Ask again later," to quote the Magic 8-ball), but for his age, especially the more advanced one he claims, he looks good, or even fantastic. No visible battle damage anymore.

If you look at the whole story, though . . . his mother lost everyone she knew, everyone she cared about, including her husband, to Season Howe's little temper tantrum. She then spent the next several hundred years trying to get revenge. Or justice. Her sons carried on the same fight for her, giving up anything that might resemble a normal life. Every human Daniel has known, until the very recent past, has aged and died on him.

And his brother, Abraham? Oh, yeah, Season killed him. Late 1880s, I think he said.

So it's no wonder he's just a little pissed, right?

More later.

K.

6

The next couple of days reminded Kerry of an extended *Survivor* episode as her roommates shared whispered conversations with one another, formed and broke alliances, and generally acted as if their world had been turned upside down. She was willing to concede that maybe it had. Daniel spent most of his time away from the apartment, not wanting to attract "undue attention," which Kerry took to be synonymous with "Season Howe."

Maybe because it had become clear that Kerry shared a bond with Daniel that the others didn't, she felt as if she were being excluded from most of the discussions. Every now and then someone would come to her, trying to sway her over to their side, but she hadn't been involved at all in the initial choosing of sides.

Still, her opinion seemed to be valued, and she had a hard time being left alone at all. When she wanted an ice-cream sandwich one evening and was about to walk to the corner to buy one, Mace insisted on joining her. She found Brandy far more solicitous than usual, offering her tea, cookies, and a sympathetic ear whenever she wanted one. It was, she thought, as if she was the key to something but she didn't even know where the door was much less what was behind it.

The basic positions were, it was true, pretty clear. Brandy and her camp thought that Daniel was some kind of charlatan, and that they should call the police on him, at the very least. Rebecca's side believed he was practically a messiah, and that they should all team up with him and do anything he asked. Kerry came down somewhere in the middle—she believed most of what Daniel had told them, but she wanted to maintain a healthy skepticism about him until she had a better idea of what he was after.

Besides Brandy and Rebecca, who had staked out positions early, the sides were vague and shifted as often as the wind. Scott kept his opinions mostly to himself, but sided with Brandy more out of default than reason. Josh flew back and forth, depending on who made the last argument, which was not even necessarily the best. Mace felt a powerful loyalty to Rebecca, with whom, against all odds, he had formed a fast friendship over the summer, but he didn't mind telling her from time to time that she was acting stupid.

Daniel hadn't, as yet, made any particular requests of the group. He had moved them from the La Jolla house, he explained, because he felt responsible for exposing them to Season's wrath, and he wanted to protect them. He hung around for the same reason, spending his days out in search of the witch, and his nights close to the apartment in case she sought them out.

The rest of the apartment was quiet one night when Daniel and Kerry sat around the second-hand kitchen table he'd scrounged from somewhere. She traced designs in the cheap linoleum tabletop with the tip of her finger while he sipped from a can of Barq's root beer. He'd been talking about some of the changes he'd seen during his long life. "In those days," he was saying, "you could walk from the Atlantic coast to the Mississippi River without ever coming out from under trees. If you were a monkey, you could make the whole trip without ever touching the ground, limb to limb. It wasn't until you reached the Great Plains and the southwestern deserts that the trees gave way to other sorts of landscapes."

"Could anyone have predicted what would happen?" Kerry asked him.

"That the population would swell and all those people would need places to live, and that those forests would be cleared to provide lumber and paper, until the land was a sea of houses instead of trees? No, I don't think so." His mouth was a grim line, and there was a sadness in his eyes that Kerry could barely fathom.

He's seen so much, she thought. She had come to believe that he was as old as he claimed and that he had abilities far beyond any she had ever conceived of.

"No," he said again. "Some people speculated, of course, that the United States—once we'd given it that name—would grow quickly. But the land, the trees, the animals, the water—we thought those things were abundant enough to last forever." He took another sip from the aluminum can. "Obviously we miscalculated." He smiled. "We should have thought to recycle our aluminum back then, I guess."

She laughed with him, which she was finding easy to do. "Yeah, why were you guys so backward?"

He finished the root beer and set the empty can down on the table. But before he could speak again, one of the bedroom doors opened and the rest of the roommates filed out, grave expressions on their faces.

When Brandy stepped forward as their spokesperson, Kerry was pretty sure she knew what was coming.

"Daniel, we've taken a vote," she began.

"I didn't vote," Kerry interrupted. "Don't I get a say in whatever this is?"

"You can vote, but your vote won't be enough to change the balance," Brandy told her. "If it had been, we'd have included you."

"Thanks for the consideration," Kerry snapped, feeling betrayed by the very people she'd thought were her friends.

"Anyway, Daniel, here's what it comes

down to. We've all upset our lives over this mess, some of us have lost our jobs, worried our parents. It's got to end. Summer's almost over anyway, and we'll all be going our separate ways. But for the rest of the summer, for as much of it as we can salvage, we'd like you gone."

There was a moment of silence. Nobody met Kerry's eyes.

"Gone?" he echoed.

"That's right. Don't come around, don't call."

"But Season—"

"None of us has ever seen Season, except Kerry. She's left us alone so far. We'll take our chances."

"You don't know what you're getting into," he warned.

"Whatever it is, you're the one got us into it," Brandy countered. "Now, we're telling you we're done with it."

Daniel glanced at Kerry, but she couldn't bring herself to hold his gaze. She looked away from him, at his pop can sitting on the table, forgotten now. "What . . . what was the vote?" she asked hesitantly.

"Four to one," Brandy answered.

Four to one. That meant . . . Kerry looked at Rebecca. The girl's huge, soft brown eyes brimmed with tears. Brandy and Mace were the only ones who appeared certain. Scott shifted his weight from foot to foot, while Josh looked at his Converse sneakers, his eyes lined with black, the studded stainless steel collar he liked to wear, when not on duty, as tight around his neck as a strangler's hands.

"Four to two," Kerry corrected. But the world tilted sharply up around her in a vertiginous spin—the overhead lights seemed to reverse on themselves, giving out black rays that fought against a pale white background, and blood roared in her ears like an express subway past an abandoned station.

Daniel shoved his chair back on the bunching carpet and stood up. "Thank you, Kerry," he said. "But majority rules, right?"

Does it have to? Kerry wondered. They'd been talking about American history, and she knew there had been times when majority hadn't ruled at all, times when the powerful forced their will upon others. And Kerry had as strong a will as anyone—"stubborn," that's what most people called it, except her mother who had always preferred "determined." Or "Bulldog," as her housemates had named her. She wasn't sure how she could force the others to change their minds, but that didn't mean she couldn't try.

Except she was unable to form a sentence with the floor spinning beneath her feet. "I'll get my things," Daniel said, apparently interpreting her confused silence as acquiescence.

He didn't, as far as she had been able to tell, have many things to get. When they'd found him in their bushes, he had only the clothes on his back. He had been living some place, though, and he had a knapsack's worth of possessions that he'd gathered from there after installing them all in this apartment. Kerry supposed that it was possible he had a house full of stuff somewhere—obviously, there was still far more that she didn't know about him than that she did. Since the apartment, shabby as it was, actually had more bedrooms than their house had, Brandy and Scott shared one, while Josh and Mace bunked together in another, Rebecca and Kerry in the third. Daniel, when he slept, did so in the living room on a worn, thrift-shop sofa, next to which he stored his leather pack. He crossed the room and picked it up now, moving with graceful economy, surely knowing that all eyes were on him.

Kerry felt her own eyes growing misty. She wasn't sure how much of that was because Rebecca was sniffling, huge round tears rolling down her pudgy cheeks, and how much was because, as briefly as Daniel had been part of her life, she would miss him. She sniffed once, determined not to cry.

"Daniel . . . ," she began, but she wasn't at all sure where she was going with it, and she let it hang there.

He looked at her, as if reading her meaning anyway. "Don't, Kerry," he said. "If you need me, I'll be there."

"But not here," Brandy chimed in.

"Not here."

"And no stalking, dude," Mace added.

"Not a chance," Daniel assured him. He hoisted the backpack onto his shoulder, took a last look around at everyone, gave a smile and a friendly wave, and walked out the door.

Kerry Profitt's diary, August 20

How many times can you lose a person that you never really got a chance to know?

7

For Mace, the whole crazy thing was just too much to cope with.

He'd lost his job the night Kerry had run out of the restaurant with Daniel. He'd been back at his station in a corner of the kitchen, washing dishes, iPod screaming The Strokes into his ear, completely unaware of what was happening until a burst of light caught his attention. His first thought was that someone was taking flash pictures, though why anyone would want to do such a thing in a busy restaurant kitchen was beyond him. But looking up, he caught a glimpse of Kerry and Daniel diving out the door, pursued by a blond with a reasonably high hotness quotient.

The whole thing was more than a little freaky. Kerry was a friend of his, though, so he dropped a stack of plates, which caught the edge of the big sink and shattered onto the floor, and ran past the stunned kitchen staff and into the parking lot. Two cars roared away. His own car was parked in an employee lot a quarter mile away. He ran for it and lit it up, but way too late—the car Kerry had jetted in was history.

When he made his way back to the kitchen, the restaurant manager, Emil Hofstadter—who Mace was pretty sure had been born John Smith, or something like it, and whose name was as phony as his Swiss accent—had been furious, though he denied having seen anything out of the ordinary. But with no Kerry to take out his anger on, he'd directed it at Mace. Knowing it was completely without justification, Mace sucked it up anyway, figuring it might help protect Kerry from any fallout. But then, a couple of hours later, when Rebecca came in and told him that Kerry had called her and said they all needed to get out of there, now—even though his shift would have been over in twenty-five minutes—Mace had gone along with her, walking out right in front of a raging Emil. He knew then that the job was history. Emil's arms were crossed over his chest and his face was the color of an eggplant, with veins standing out on his forehead like they were about to burst.

So he'd given up the job, and willingly. Not happily, mind you—he didn't have money in the family like Scott and Brandy, or an insurance settlement like Kerry, and had to work for what he got. But friends came first, even when they had only become friends over the course of the summer. Besides, when Rebecca directed those puppy-dog browns at him, he didn't know how to say no.

But the whole crazy deal with Daniel was just too much to put up with. Even though Brandy had won the battle, and the man had been exiled from the apartment—which he had paid for, which meant, Mace supposed, that he could show up again at any time—Mace still wasn't comfortable hanging around any more. Occult stuff really gave him the chills. He didn't even like horror movies, unless they were so ridiculously slasher-ific that there was no way to believe in them. But he thought that messing around with magic was just asking for trouble, the kind that he didn't want to have to cope with.

He didn't *believe* in magic—who would, in their right mind? He figured the stuff Daniel had shown them was nothing but trickery of some kind. And even though Kerry swore some kind of magical battle had gone on in the kitchen that night, there had been no damage left behind and he hadn't seen it, had only observed some bright lights. That didn't mean he was comfortable with it, though.

So the morning after the final confrontation with Daniel, he got up early and packed up Susie, his baby blue Lincoln Continental. He said adios to his summer friends, after coffee and churros from the taco stand on the corner of Palm, with lots of hugs and handshakes. Rebecca cried, as she would, and pulled him close to her, and the curves and valleys of her lush figure beneath her loose clothes made him think twice about what he was doing. But then he saw Kerry, ivory pale, green eyes looking bruised and bloodshot from worrying about Daniel, he guessed, and knew that of all of them, she'd have the hardest time giving up the strange old man—and he her—and if the guy was going to come back into their lives, Mace just didn't want to be there for it.

Susie started right up, as she always did. Rebecca stood on the sidewalk and waved until he was out of sight. He cranked the tape deck—damn thing was built before CD players; that and the gas mileage were Susie's main drawbacks—and headed for Interstate 5, which would connect with the I-8, which would merge with the I-10 and take him all the way to Las Cruces. From there the I-70 would lead home to Clovis. In minutes he was on the freeway, and he lowered the window a few inches so the wind would blow on his face as he drove. To Mace, that was one of the joys of a road trip—wind in your face, tunes blaring, blacktop spooling out behind you like film running through a projector.

He'd only gone a few miles, though—hadn't even reached the I-8, which ran east-west across the bottom edge of the southwest—when Susie started to act up. Susie, for whom he cared as if she were a precious thing, started to bump and knock and rattle like she'd been inhabited by a family of poltergeists. There was no reason she should have any problems, given how carefully and meticulously he maintained her, but he couldn't ignore the noises and the shuddering that got worse with each passing mile.

With a curse and an angry slap on the steering wheel, he gave up and pulled off at the next exit. Downtown San Diego loomed ahead of him, the I-8 a few miles beyond that. But here, off to the side of the freeway, there was only a vacant industrial area—warehouses and a railroad track and then a stretch of sloughs and shipyards close to the shore. Mace pulled Susie over in the shade of one of the warehouses and killed the engine.

He sat behind the wheel listening to her tick for a few minutes, letting the engine cool a little. Inside, he fumed, but he tried to keep that from her. A car was a sentient being, or close to it, he believed, and you didn't want to let one know when you were genuinely mad at it. Talking nice was almost always preferable. He apologized for having struck the steering wheel, and then popped the hood.

He couldn't have said where the woman came from. The neighborhood had been deserted, the only sound the steady rush of the nearby freeway, the only smell the sour, fecund stink of the standing water between here and the ocean. But between the time he opened the hood and glanced inside—to see an engine that looked just as cherry as it ever did—and the time that it took for him to go back into the car to get a rag to wipe his hands on, she had come up behind him. He stood up, rubbing at a spot of oil on his left index finger, and she was just standing there, a dozen feet away, looking at him. Tall, blond, wearing faded jeans and a black tank top and an expression like a stern librarian giving her last warning.

"Where is he?" she demanded. As soon as she spoke, Mace realized who she had to be. "Season," Daniel had called her. Mace had seen her before, in the kitchen that night, though only from behind. He recognized the honeyed hair, however, her statuesque carriage, her muscular form.

And anyway, who else could it be? This is just too perfect.

"I don't know what you're talking about," he replied.

"Just tell me where to find Daniel," she said, "and you'll be fine."

He started to speak again, to deny that he knew who she meant, but she narrowed her eyes and parted her lips just a little and he knew that it was pointless. He didn't know *how* she knew—didn't want to know, for that matter. But she did.

"I have no idea," he said. "He was hanging around, but we kicked him out last night. I don't know where he went."

She started toward him then, walking slowly, with pretend casualness, but he didn't trust her intentions for a second. "Let's just see about that," she said. Visions of aliens with mind probes leapt into his head, and he knew that the last thing he wanted was this woman, whatever she was, rooting around in his thoughts.

He ran for Susie's open door and hurled himself inside, grabbing and twisting the key that still hung in her ignition. The engine grumbled but caught, and he yanked the door shut as he stomped on the gas. The blond stood in the roadway before him, coming toward the car as if she intended to stop it with her own body and tug him out. Mace wasn't thinking clearly, wasn't processing. *Get out of here,* that's what went through his mind, over and over. *Get out of here. Get out—*

But she was in the way and she didn't look

like she was moving, and anyway she was trouble, anyone could see that . . .

—*of here.*

. . . and instead of swerving around her, he turned the wheel ever so slightly, and pointed Susie's enormous bulk right *at* her.

The big car ate up the feet between them. He braced himself for the inevitable impact.

Which didn't come.

He reached the spot where she should have been, but she didn't seem to be there any more. It took him a moment before he realized it wasn't that she had moved, but that *he* had—his direction of travel had changed. Instead of pushing through her toward the open road, he was hurtling *toward* the cement block wall of the nearest warehouse.

Mace pawed at the wheel and started to correct his course, but even as he did, he knew it was too late. He was moving too fast, had come too close. The wall loomed huge in his windshield, and then—

8

"Mace is dead."

Daniel stood in the doorway, his face drawn, looking worse than at any time Kerry had seen him since that first night. This time it wasn't physical pain he felt, she believed, but emotional. He had come to deliver bad news. And he experienced the hurt of that news himself, maybe even some complicity.

"I'm so sorry," he went on, filling the silence when she didn't say anything. "I feel just terrible."

Confirming her theory. "Did you have anything to do with it?" *Cold,* she thought, *but necessary.*

"No. Yes." He looked at the ground, then back at her, eyes wide and solemn. "Just that . . . while he was allied with the rest of you, he was under my protection. Once he made the decision to leave, he slipped from my sphere of influence. She must have been waiting for something like that, for the scent of any of you. She must have caught up to him. It's the only thing that could have happened."

Somehow the explanation, perfunctory as it was, made it all more real to her, and she herself turning numb. "How . . ." she began, but couldn't finish. She swallowed hard and stepped aside, wordlessly inviting him in.

"He had pulled off the freeway in an industrial area, for no reason that I can discern, and drove straight into a warehouse wall. The speed and force must have been incredible. Do you want to know more?"

"I . . . want to know everything," she said. Josh, Brandy, and Scott were at work. Rebecca had lost her job at Seaside when she and Mace bailed from the kitchen and she had gone down to the nearby branch library for some books. Kerry knew that they'd all have questions, lots of them, and she wanted to be able to answer whatever came up.

"The force of impact drove the engine

block through the passenger compartment," Daniel elaborated. "He would have been killed instantly. I'm sure he didn't suffer."

"But . . . if it was her . . . why? Would she have . . . tortured him?"

Daniel shrugged, but his face remained grim as he considered the possibility. "Maybe. I doubt it, though. The way they found him . . . if she had had any time with him, I don't think he would have been in the car."

Kerry flopped down on the couch, suddenly feeling unsteady on her feet. A darkness seemed to close in around her, but she didn't know if it was actual or spiritual. Or if it really mattered, in the long run. People died—in the thrillers she liked to read, and her own parents had died—but she had never known of a violent death before, and the thought of it staggered her, made her feel sick. "What, is she just evil? Why would she do that?"

Daniel sat beside her and put a hand on her knee. "I'm sure she's still trying to find me, to use my association with you all to track me and finish me off. I've regained most of my strength since our last serious encounter, but if she still expects that I'm weakened, she'll want to press her advantage." He looked away from her, at the plastered ceiling. "Which makes his death my fault," he said, sounding very somber. "One more in a long line."

Kerry felt that she should argue with him, should claim somehow that Mace took his own chances by leaving. But that wasn't right, she realized, since he had no way of knowing what might have been in store for him if he left. None of them had known that they were still under Daniel's protection, so how could they be aware of what might happen if they left it? No, he was right—Mace's death was on him.

On him . . . and Season Howe.

"As to whether she's evil," Daniel continued, "the answer is very definitely yes. I thought I'd made that clear."

"I guess I don't understand what her game is," Kerry said. Daniel's hand still rested on her knee, and it was getting to the point where she'd have to acknowledge it with a squeeze of her own or shift away from it with whatever message that would send, or it would become like the elephant in the room, impossible to pretend wasn't there. But then probably she was only dwelling on it to distract herself from the fact of Mace's death—the real elephant in the room. "What is she after?"

Apparently he caught on to the knee situation too. He gave a final pat and took his hand away, raising it and his other one chest high in a gesture of uncertainty. "Who knows? I like to think that by keeping the pressure on her, keeping her on the run, I've prevented her from putting any grand plans into motion. But bad things happen every day, everywhere on Earth. Might she be responsible for some of those? Of course."

Kerry rubbed her eyes, as if that would help her discern Season's motives. "But you don't have any proof that she's still up to bad things?" she asked. "Nothing you can pin on her recently?"

"Murdering Mace," he reminded her.

"Yeah," Kerry agreed, feeling the numbness overtake her again. There had just been too much going on emotionally this last week or so. She hadn't been sleeping well, hadn't been eating right. It wore on her, and she was afraid that she was simply shutting down, one part at a time. "Yeah, there's that."

• • •

Josh had just parked a Lexus at the north lot and was starting to hoof it back to the valet station when one of his coworkers, Kevin, pulled up to the curb nearby in a gigantic black Escalade. Kevin rolled down the driver's window and leaned his head out. He was big and shaggy, with the sunstreaked blond locks of the surfer he was. He mostly worked nights because he preferred the morning waves. "Dude!" he called. Josh jogged over to him.

"What's up?"

"Hey, you knew that guy Mace, right? Dishwasher?"

"Yeah, he's my—" Kevin's use of the past tense suddenly struck him, and Josh felt his insides turn to hot liquid. "What do you mean?"

"Dude, he got killed," Kevin said casually. "There's some cops askin' for anyone who knew him. Detectives, I guess, in suits. They started with valets because we're right out in front, but it looks like they're gonna work their way around."

"Killed how?" Josh demanded. His legs felt like pipe cleaners, like they were about to buckle under his weight.

"I don't know," Kevin answered. "They

were into asking questions, not answerin' 'em."

The specifics of it, Josh knew, weren't really the important thing. The fact was, Mace was dead—unless this whole deal was some colossal misunderstanding, which seemed unlikely. Mace was not the kind of guy to whom Josh would normally be drawn, but over the summer they had become friends anyway, and to think his life had been suddenly snuffed . . .

Then another thought burst into his consciousness, and he believed—no, he *knew*—that this was somehow related to those freaking witches, Season and Daniel. Somehow Mace had been caught in their crossfire and had paid the price for it.

Which meant that any of them could be next.

Scott and Brandy, he thought suddenly. They were working today too, and they had to be found and warned. If the cops could find them, so could the witch.

Without a parting word to Kevin, he broke into a panicked run. Scott could be anywhere, but Brandy would only be one place—the hotel's front desk. It would be the second place the cops would go, after the valet stand. He needed to call her, get her out of there. As he ran, he tore off his red valet's vest, not wanting to be easily recognizable to the police. He hurled it to the ground, followed it with his bow tie. Now he was just a guy in a white shirt and black pants, running full tilt across the resort grounds, digging a cell phone from his pocket as he did.

Kerry Profitt's diary, August 21

Much to my astonishment, Rebecca didn't cry when we told her about Mace.

I'd have put money on it. The girl is such a soft touch she wants to take in every stray dog, cat, or homeless person we see on the streets, of which, especially that last one, there are plenty. But then, San Diego in summer? Relatively mild, no humidity, not too bad in the bug department (I haven't suffered a mosquito bite since I got here, which is more than I could say for Illinois in the summer). If I was homeless, which so far is only a borderline possibility, there aren't many places I'd rather live.

She said, changing the subject.

Then again, I didn't cry either. Mace Winston, not my favorite person (can you say that about the dead?) was gone, and I felt—and feel—just horrible. I'm sure

Rebecca feels the same way. I've never seen her look so sad as when she came in the door, a bunch of library books under her arm, and we told her. But no tears fell. They will tonight, later, I expect. She's still out in the living room as I write this, and I have a feeling that when we're both in here tonight, with the lights out, there are going to be tears on both our pillows.

Mostly what I feel is empty. And angry. As if Mace, who as I pointed out was not my best friend in life, has left a giant hole inside me through his absence. And even though I never expected to see him again anyway after he drove into the sunrise, the idea that he's not out there anymore, the idea that I couldn't call him or see him even if I wanted to, is somehow too horrible to really process.

I'm sure the police notified his parents. Mace had ID on him, they knew who he was. Fortunately not where he was living most recently, because a whole lot of questions could come up that we have no interest in answering. I was a little surprised to find that, on that question, at least, Brandy and I were in agreement.

More later.

K.

Later, Kerry heard a clatter on the outside stairs, which meant that Scott, Brandy, and Josh were home, earlier than anticipated, and the heavy footfalls indicated that they were upset too. She tossed a wan smile Daniel's way—he was still on the couch, but she had paced for a while and then settled in a chair—and waited for the inevitable. Rebecca heard the noise too, and drifted in from the bedroom she and Kerry shared, exchanging glances with both Kerry and Daniel.

When the door flew open, Brandy was the first one inside. She took in the scene quickly. "So you've heard," she said.

"We've heard," Kerry confirmed.

Brandy dropped her purse unceremoniously to the floor; she always seemed to carry the approximate weight of a small city with her at any given time, Kerry thought. "This is your fault," she said, boring in on Daniel with her glare.

"You're right, Brandy," Daniel agreed. "I am so terribly sorry. It was because of my association with you that Season Howe killed Mace."

Scott and Josh crowded in behind Brandy, who had stopped just a couple of feet in front of the door, and had her arms folded, legs wide. *An aggressive stance,* Kerry thought, *like she's spoiling for a fight.* Sunlight splashed in through a part in the curtain, giving her caramel-colored skin a soft glow.

"Do you know for sure it was her?" Scott asked.

Daniel gave a little shrug. "I didn't witness it, if that's what you mean. But in my heart, yes, I'm certain. Unless you think Mace would have intentionally driven into a wall."

Scott pulled his glasses off and wiped them on the tail of his tan uniform shirt. "That doesn't sound like him."

"Not at all," Josh agreed. He squeezed behind Scott and planted himself on the floor, legs crossed, back against the wall. Kerry wouldn't have believed he could be any paler than his usual paper-white, but he seemed almost gray now. "Mace was, like, the least suicidal guy I've ever known. And a good driver besides. And even if he would kill himself, which he wouldn't, he'd never do anything to hurt that car."

"No," Brandy echoed. "He wouldn't do that."

"It was Season, then," Scott said, replacing his glasses and blinking behind them. He sounded like he was trying to convince himself, and was slowly coming around to that position. "She killed him."

"That's right," Kerry found herself saying. "That's what Daniel's been telling us."

"But if it wasn't for you he'd still be alive," Brandy declared.

Daniel looked at her calmly. "Most likely, yes."

"And we'd all still have our jobs," Josh said.

Kerry had already noticed that they were home early, but now she realized that Josh wasn't wearing his vest or tie, nor had he carried them in. Brandy still had on the conservative gray skirt and tight short-sleeved top she'd worn that morning, and Scott was in his groundskeeper uniform, but neither of them had work accessories that could as easily be abandoned as Josh's. "You didn't all quit, did you?" she asked.

"Effectively, since we just walked away from them," Brandy said, her dark eyes smoldering.

"It was either that or talk to the cops. As it is, I'm sure they'll be calling our families pretty soon, trying to track us down. We're in a serious situation here."

"The police were already there?" Kerry asked, surprised.

"Looking for us, apparently," Brandy replied. "There's an investigation into Mace's death."

"That makes sense," Daniel said. "It just doesn't look like an accident."

"So you saw where it happened?" Scott asked him. He still stood, a half step behind Brandy.

"I did," Daniel answered. "After the fact. I had a sense that something had happened, something involving one of you—"

"Then why weren't you able to stop it?" Brandy demanded.

"It was *after* the fact," Daniel repeated. "As I explained to Kerry and Rebecca, by leaving the rest of you behind, Mace took himself outside my protection."

Brandy shook her head. "There shouldn't even *be* protection," she fumed. "We told you to leave us alone! What part of that don't you get?"

"I couldn't, not completely," Daniel said by way of defense. "I had involved you in something dangerous. Without my protection, what happened to Mace would have happened to all of you by now. Unless—"

"There's an unless?" Rebecca asked, her voice so high it squeaked.

"Unless you give me up," he finished. "If you tell Season where to find me, then she might let you live."

"But Mace didn't . . . ," Kerry began.

"You had sent me away. Mace had no idea where to find me. Even if he'd wanted to save his own life, he wouldn't have been able to."

Brandy slumped as if she'd been deflated. "So really, I . . ."

Scott grabbed her shoulders from behind, like he was trying to keep her from sinking into the floor. "Brandy, no!"

"But it's true," she said quietly. "If I hadn't insisted we make Daniel leave, Mace would still be alive."

"Possibly," Scott countered.

"No," she snapped, turning on him. "I was the one who pushed and pushed to get Daniel out of here. If I hadn't—"

"Scott's right, Brandy," Daniel said, trying to console her. "There's no way to know what might have happened. Mace might have gone anyway, and then he still would have been outside my protection. He could have given me up, told her to find me here. But that doesn't guarantee that she wouldn't have killed him anyway."

"I guess." She sat down on the floor, with Scott helping her down. He remained beside her, like a bodyguard. "But still . . ."

"You can never know what might have happened, Brandy," Daniel assured her. "Or what's going to happen. The best you can do is try to make the right decisions when they present themselves."

"So what's the best decision now?" Josh asked. "I mean, we're basically screwed, right? The cops are looking for us, we've lost our jobs, and this Season witch is going to try to run us down one by one."

"Unless . . . ," Daniel began.

"Unless what?" Kerry asked.

"Unless," he continued, "we take the fight back to her."

9

Daniel didn't have much in the way of a plan, Kerry learned. *But then, if he had, he might not have spent the last three centuries chasing her from place to place.* He admitted as much over fast-food burgers and milk shakes in the apartment that he had moved back into, taking the now-vacant bed that had been used by Mace.

"Season's survival skills are well-honed," he told them. "She's hard to get the drop on, virtually impossible to ambush. Every now and then I get a lead on where she is, but even then, she's so much more powerful than me that I have to plan my strategy carefully, and that's just to give me a fighting chance. I can't say that I've ever had the advantage."

"Can you beat her?" Scott asked. His

neatly trimmed collegiate hair, Kerry noticed, was starting to grow a bit long and unruly. "Or is it just not even worth trying?"

"Am I spinning my wheels?" Daniel rephrased Scott's question. "I like to think I'm not. But then I suppose the same is true of anyone on a long, fruitless hunt. Was Ahab wasting his time chasing the white whale all over creation? A lot of people would say yes." He took a deep breath and blew it out slowly. There was, Kerry thought, a sadness in his eyes while he considered the question. "Certainly there are other things I could have done with my life. I could have helped more people, I suppose. Saved more lives in some other capacity. But I believed—I continue to believe—that Season is a threat, a real danger, to everyone whose path she crosses. She's not going away on her own, so someone has to step in and deal with her."

"That's not exactly what I meant," Scott said, his elbows on the cheap table as he wrested a fry from its paper bag. "I meant more, like, can you take her on, or is it pointless to try? But since you bring it up—not to be too nosy or anything—but just how long can you guys live?"

Daniel smiled briefly. "Got it," he answered with a chuckle. "I didn't mean to be evasive. Short answer, this time—yes, I believe I can take her. Not easily, as I've mentioned, and probably not one-on-one in a fair fight. But I've long since given up the idea of fighting her fairly. Question two—I'm not entirely sure. I knew a witch once who claimed to be well over a thousand. He said that he'd narrowly escaped death at the Battle of Hastings, and when I knew him he looked every single one of those thousand and some years. He died shortly after that, of natural causes. Or at least that's what I was told."

"So the fact that Season was an adult when she wrecked your town doesn't necessarily mean that she's likely to die of old age any time soon," Brandy suggested.

"You've seen her, Kerry," Daniel pointed out. "She look like she's on her deathbed to you?"

"I wish," Kerry replied. "But, no. I could only hope to look that good when I'm thirty-five."

Josh had been staring blankly at a corner of the room, and Kerry wasn't sure he had even been tracking the conversation. But now he swiveled his head, neck stiff as if it needed oiling, and fixed his gaze on Daniel. Outside, the sun had gone away, and the glow from the overhead light in the kitchen left the table half dark. "How do we off her, man?" Josh asked. "That's what this is all about, right? How do we freaking kill her?"

Kerry shuddered to hear the question phrased so bluntly. Josh was right, of course. And he had been closest to Mace—well, he and Rebecca. But Rebecca wasn't the kind of person who would think along those lines, under any circumstance. Josh, though—the set of his chin and the hardness of his eyes reminded Kerry of a character from the hard-boiled movies he loved so much. *He could be turned into a killer,* she realized. *Maybe he already has been, and now he just needs the opportunity.*

Daniel shrugged. "First we find her," he said, as if it was that easy. "Then *I* kill her. Not you. Not any of you. You wouldn't stand a chance against Season Howe."

"Try me," Josh said.

"I'm serious, Josh," Daniel assured him. "Not a chance. She wouldn't even break a sweat against you. But . . ." He paused before he went on, as if choosing his words carefully. Perhaps debating whether to say them at all. ". . . you can help. You can track her down."

"How?" Rebecca asked. "Wouldn't that, like, make us even bigger targets? Like Mace was?"

"Mace was outside my protection, so he was no longer shielded from her," Daniel explained. "It's not a physical thing, not a matter of distance or anything like that. Mace left the rest of you behind, and by doing so he opted out of my protection spell. But the rest of you—you could walk right up to Season, and she'd never know you were the ones who helped me. As long as you all work together." He looked at Kerry. "Except you, Kerry. She's seen you. She can't sense where you are, but if she sees you again, she'll know you."

"I understand," Kerry said.

"But if we find her, then what?" Scott asked. "Aren't we back to square one? We have to let you know where she is, and then you have to get there and somehow do battle against a superior opponent."

"Sounds so easy when you put it that way."

Daniel was smiling when he said it, but his grin didn't look particularly mirthful.

Under Daniel's direction—and more significantly, he promised, his protection—they split up the next morning to go look for Season Howe. Kerry was impressed by his visual aid: he generated, or rather, projected, an almost-photographic image of Season in the inch of black coffee left at the bottom of Scott's cup, clear enough that even those who had never seen the witch in person would recognize her. Daniel didn't want to let the image last for long for fear, he said, that she would somehow be able to lock onto it. So he told everyone to take a good look, and then he stirred the coffee and the image went away.

Season liked crowds, Daniel had said, and transient populations, where strangers weren't unusual. So to cover the most ground possible, they paired off—Scott and Brandy, of course, Rebecca and Josh, Daniel and Kerry. Rebecca and Josh decided they'd scope out downtown San Diego, look into the coffee shops and boutiques of the Gaslamp Quarter and the stores of Horton Plaza. Scott and Brandy—who, since Mace died, was willing to go along even though he still hadn't come around to believing in Daniel—went to scout the beaches. Daniel and Kerry knew that it was impossible for six people to cover the entire city—plus there was always the chance, though Daniel insisted it was remote, that Season had already moved on—but they also knew they had to make the best possible effort. So Kerry and Daniel went to a place where they knew there would be crowds: the San Diego Zoo.

At Daniel's suggestion, everyone had contacted their parents or other adult caretakers—in Kerry's case, it had been a simple e-mail to Uncle Marsh's work account, which Kerry knew would suffice—to let them know that there had been a change of address and phone number, but that they were okay. Since most of their folks used their mobile phones anyway, the change wouldn't be a big deal to them. Kerry had rarely spoken to her aunt and uncle since she'd been in California, but then again, she rarely talked to them even when they lived in the same house. Rebecca was close to her parents and three brothers, as were Scott and Brandy to their families, but Josh almost never mentioned his, and Kerry was pretty sure only his mother was still alive.

The zoo was nearly always busy, but on a warm summer afternoon it was almost over-whelmingly so. The line from the ticket booths extended most of the way to the parking lot. Kerry thought she'd die of sunstroke by the time they got inside, the sun not being a friend to her fair skin. But Daniel told her to wait in the shade while he stood in line, and in a few minutes they had passed through the turnstiles. Inside, the air had a different quality—the exhaust of cars and tour buses was left behind on the other side of the walls, and they moved into a world of exotic scents—scores of plants mixing with the rich, pungent odors of the birds and animals that surrounded them. The scenery was a riot of colors—the Hawaiian shirts and casual clothes of zoo-goers battling for supremacy with the bright plumage of the flamingoes near the front entrance. Daniel didn't add much to the display in his jeans and dark blue T-shirt, but Kerry had opted for a crimson-and-white striped rugby shirt, with the long sleeves pushed up, and white hip huggers.

"Flamingoes were used as the hieroglyphic

symbol for the color red, in ancient Egypt," Daniel told her as they threaded their way through the crowd. "And to represent the reincarnation of Ra, the sun god."

Kerry studied his face, looking for signs of age that weren't there. "You're not *that* old, though," she said.

Daniel laughed. "No, not that old. Just old enough to have picked up lots of totally useless information along the way."

"Not totally useless," Kerry argued. "There's the sheer entertainment value. Not to mention the possibility of scoring big on TV game shows."

He smiled, but he was standing up on the balls of his feet, scanning the crowd for any sign of Season. "Yeah, I guess that's true," he admitted.

"Speaking of cash," she pressed. "How do you survive, anyway? You don't seem to be gainfully employed, not that I can tell."

Daniel looked away from the crowd long enough to meet her gaze for a moment. Just under his right jaw line, where she usually didn't notice it, was a scar like a half-curled worm against his skin. She had meant to ask about it before, but never had. "Turns out if you take the long-term view—and I mean, really long term—the stock market isn't a bad place to keep some money. And even a bank account will do pretty well after a hundred years or so of collecting interest."

"What about government records? Social Security, the IRS, stuff like that?" She'd been too absorbed in the craziness of the hunt to give much thought to such mundane questions before, but now that they'd occurred to her, she couldn't stop the flow.

"Nothing that can't be doctored with a simple spell," Daniel explained.

"And doctors? Doesn't your family doctor wonder if you never age?"

"We tend to take care of our own. Don't have much need of doctors." He touched her arm. "And sometimes an angel of mercy appears from nowhere when you need her most."

She felt herself blushing, and turned away. But then she reached up, almost as if she couldn't stop herself, and touched the curled scar. "What's this one? Seems like that might have needed some medical attention."

His face changed slightly, as if a shadow had passed over it, and he rubbed the spot she had just touched. "I could have removed it," he said. His voice had turned to steel. "But that one I got the day she killed Abraham."

"Your brother," Kerry remembered. Twins, he'd said, born shortly after Season had destroyed their town.

"That's right." They had stopped walking, and the flow or humanity coursed around them like a river around boulders. A woman pushing twins in a stroller shot them a dirty look, as if they had intentionally blocked her path, but then picked a side and moved on. "Season did that, with an enchanted blade she carried in those days. Nearly killed me. Took me out of action long enough for her to finish Abe. He was trying to help me, and she cut him too. Left us both for dead. Unlucky for her. She should have finished me off then."

He touched the spot again and then shook his hand, like he could shake off the memory as easily as a few drops of water. Kerry felt bad for bringing up something so obviously painful, and thought she should change the subject. "Why here?" she asked, starting to walk again. Signs ahead of them pointed toward the children's zoo and the Absolutely Apes exhibit. "Why would she be at the zoo?"

"She would be here, or at the beach or the mall or some other place, because her whole goal is not to stand out. She is probably living in a hotel, although it's possible she found a summer rental. Either way, there would be someone—neighbors, hotel staff, a cleaning service—who would notice if she spent these warm summer days holed up in the room. She wants to look like every other out-of-towner here for the season, so she goes to places like this, even if she has no special interest in them."

"And you can't just magically track her down?"

"No more than she can track me, or you while you're under my protection. I've got counterspells, and so does she. If we see each other, then it's war. But if I can't find her before she leaves town, then I've got to start all over."

They made the turn toward the apes exhibit area, for no particular reason that she could determine. There was a part of Kerry that enjoyed just walking through the zoo with a handsome, interesting man. She wished there didn't have to be some kind of epic death hunt going on to darken the day. But at the same time, she knew it was the death hunt that had brought them together, and it remained the main thing they had in common.

"Do you ever get tired of it?" she asked. "Just want to give it up and let her go?"

Again, he stopped in his tracks. Kerry was starting to feel like the queen of hurtful questions. "You don't have to answer that," she said quickly. "It was over the line. I'm sorry."

"It's okay." He took her upper arms in his hands and held on tightly until she thought he might leave bruise marks. "I don't feel like I have to hide anything from you, Kerry. I don't quite know why that is, yet. But I kind of like it. I hope that doesn't scare you."

The only answer that came to her was the honest one. "Yeah, it does, a little. But I'll try to cope."

"The truth is, I get tired of it every day, and every day there are times when I want to give up. But I never do."

"Why not?" *You just have to push,* she

thought, even as the words left her mouth. *You big dope.*

"Honestly?" Daniel looked toward the sun, and blinked a couple of times. "I don't know what I'd do with myself. Daytime TV gets pretty dull after a few decades."

The zoo was a big strikeout, Season-wise. Brandy and Scott washed out too. As did, need I say, Rebecca and Josh. No Season, no Season, and no Season. Not that, in a city the size of San Diego, with more millions than I can remember, but several of them, it's an easy task to find a single person who doesn't especially want to be found. And as Daniel put it, better twelve eyes looking for her than two—especially since she's no doubt looking for us, too, and whoever spots the other first has the advantage.

Can't argue with the reasoning. Of course, to take it a step or two further, twelve hundred eyes would be better yet. Twelve thousand, and maybe there'd be a chance of finding her. This needle-in-the-haystack routine seems so, I don't know, eighteenth century somehow. Like we ought to be able to Google her instead of just looking.

Which, by the way, I just did. There's a hockey player named Howe who's had several good seasons, and likewise some squash news. No witchy stuff, though. So I guess, as Daniel told me while we walked past the big cats (side note—the snow leopards are spectacular!), she has done a good job of maintaining a low profile.

What is most amazing to me is that this works, he says. The low-tech thing, I mean. He has found her before, several times. Done her some damage, too, he says. Of course, she's done the same to him. Many clinches, no knockouts. Sports page girl today, that's me.

Actually, not, so don't ask why the various jock references. I might recognize Tiger Woods or Michael Jordan on the street, and not many guys can carry off bicycle shorts like Lance Armstrong, but that is, I confess, about the extent of my sports smarts.

I'm frustrated, of course, by the lack of forward momentum of our day—the first real day of what I presume to be many (at least until school beckons and we have to go our separate ways) of hunting Season Howe. But the truth is, it wasn't a bad day at all. I got to roam the zoo, and then the open spaces of Balboa Park as well as its museums and walkways, with Daniel. Who, as it turns out, is full of stories. Living three hundred years would give one plenty of material, I guess. But I sometimes have a hard time remembering what I did last week, and he's coming up with bits like the time, a hundred years ago, when he sat in a dark nickelodeon in New York and watched *The Great Train Robbery*, one of the first movies ever made.

Well, I guess I might remember something like that too. Having spent my "formative years" not exactly going to a ton of movies, I think I remember all the ones I've seen in theaters. Cried at *Titanic,* but at the wrong parts. Laughed at *My Big Fat Greek Wedding,* ditto. Guess I'm just culturally illiterate.

But the point is, walking around with Daniel, being entertained by his stories, even as we kept our eyes open for any sign of the big bad witch of the west, was nice. Balboa Park is as beautiful a spot as one could hope for. It all helped drive horrible thoughts of Mace from my mind, and I hope that somehow, wherever he is, he's found some peace. Being with Daniel felt easy, comfortable, even though I haven't known him for long and he is as different from me—being essentially immortal, many-powered and all—as it's possible to be.

All the crazy witch stuff? Turns out when you're faced with it, right in front of you, it's not so hard to believe. A month ago—two weeks ago—I would've sworn that it was all bogus. Today I'll swear till I'm blue in the face (and just what does that old cliché mean, anyway?) that it's true, that there are people—witches—among us with abilities far beyond our imagining.

I asked Daniel, while we walked and searched,

about Wiccans. I think the way I phrased it was less than charitable, something like, "so those people who sit around in circles and worship trees and stuff—are they just wannabes? Do they even know that witches like you and Season really exist, and is that what they aspire to?"

But Daniel is, apparently, kinder than I. "A few of them are," he told me. "Aware of us, I mean. Very few. To others, we're nothing more than whispers, rumors, maybe legends, if that. They aren't necessarily trying to become like us, or even thinking that's a possibility. It isn't quite as if they're acolytes. But their activities can help to power us, like we're batteries, recharged by the forces they release into the ether. So they do us a major service. And much of what they do is effective, as far as it goes. Spells to find love or employment, or to help friends through difficult situations: these can all work quite well if carried out correctly."

Okay, the colon I put in there? I made it up. Don't know if that's what he intended, or even if I'm quoting verbatim. He could probably quote something Abraham Lincoln told him in 1862 (kidding, he never met Lincoln, he says), but I don't have that particular skill.

Point is, something about Daniel—maybe

because of his special abilities—has made him remarkable in other ways too. He has an astonishing memory, and my guess is that he's just developed his mental faculties in ways most people can't even comprehend. So living for centuries just enhances his recall instead of—as I suspect would happen to me—jumbling experiences together.

Hey, I've been to Disneyland and seen the animatronic Lincoln. If I'd been alive in the 1860s, I probably would think I'd seen the real one.

I pummeled him with questions, over the course of the day. Who he had met, what he had seen. Finally, he told me he kept journals, and he'd let me read them if I was interested. I think it was a ploy to shut me up.

Didn't work.

But I'm still going to read them. How cool is that?

More later.

K.

10

The day after that, they rotated partners and continued the hunt. Kerry found herself paired with Rebecca. She felt an unexpected pang of sorrow at not getting another day with Daniel, who teamed up with Scott, while Brandy and Josh went out together. But she understood the reasoning. If the same two people searched together every time, Daniel suggested, they'd fall into patterns of looking, and maybe become complacent. If they were changed up frequently, they'd be more likely to remain alert and aware. Anyway, she liked Rebecca so she had no real problem with it, just a sense of longing to be with Daniel.

They spent a long day mall-crawling, figuring a woman who looked as good and dressed as nicely as Season Howe would probably be a serious shopper. They started south, at Plaza Bonita, and worked their way north, through Horton Plaza, Mission Valley, and its more upscale neighbor, Fashion Valley; east as far as Grossmont and Parkway Plaza; then up to La Jolla's University Town Center. Each mall seemed to have its own personality, its own core group of shoppers, in spite of the fact that most had the same national chain stores. They saw, throughout their day, a lot of attractive blondes.

Rebecca also saw at Mission Valley a pair of turquoise drop earrings she just had to have. She was wearing a blue chambray work shirt open over a white-blue tank, the tails tied across her belly, with a sky blue and green-and-yellow batik skirt. The turquoise looked like it had been plucked from the ground especially for her.

What they didn't see was Season.

Kerry had seen Rebecca sad, but she'd never seen her anything resembling grumpy before. Driving home from UTC in the Honda Civic Daniel had acquired for them was the closest the girl had come, in Kerry's memory. "This sucks more than anything,"

Rebecca groused, thumping the steering wheel for emphasis. "I've been trying to think of something that sucks worse than this, and I just can't. I mean, how many stores are there in San Diego county? Thousands? A hundred thousand? How are we supposed to find Season in the middle of all that? Why do we live in such a materialistic society, anyway? If this was a simple village of hunter-gatherers, we'd have come across her long before now."

"If we see her, we see her," Kerry countered. "If we don't, we don't. But if we don't see her and she sees us, we're going to regret it."

"Yeah, but . . ." Rebecca didn't finish the thought.

"I know," Kerry sympathized. "I feel the same way, Beck. We just have to keep trying."

"For how long, Kerry? Are we in this for the rest of our lives?"

"I don't think so," Kerry said. She wasn't entirely sure herself, though. She couldn't see the hunt lasting forever, even though it had already gone on for many lifetimes. "From what Daniel says, I think it's just a summer thing. Season will move on after that, and we'll be able to split up, go back to our own lives."

"And she won't keep looking for us?"

Let's hope, Kerry thought. "I figure she's got other things on her mind. She'll keep an eye out for Daniel. But I expect we'll be okay."

"But you can't be sure," Rebecca challenged.

"No, of course not. Not a hundred percent."

They were just about to pass by the off-ramp that led into La Jolla when an idea flashed into Kerry's head. "Rebecca!" she shouted. "Turn off here."

Rebecca cranked the wheel to the right and shot off the exit, cutting off another car that blared its horn at her. The look on her face was one of near-panic. "Why?"

"Just a thought," Kerry said. "I didn't mean to startle you. I just figured we should swing by the old house, while we're out this way. If Season's looking for us, she might be staking it out."

"So if she is, should we go there?"

"She's never seen you," Kerry reminded her. "I'll keep a low profile. Just one pass."

"Okay. . . ." Rebecca didn't sound convinced, but she drove toward the house they had once shared, in the part of town known as Bird Rock. Kerry wasn't sure what to expect when they got there. The place was full of memories, most happy, some frightening, as when they'd first discovered Daniel. And, of course, memories of poor, lost Mace that weighed on her like a lead blanket.

When they reached their old block, Kerry scrunched down low in the passenger seat, so that only her eyes and the top of her head showed over the window. "Drive slow," she instructed. Rebecca's knuckles were white on the wheel, and there was a bit of a shake to her arms. "We'll be fine." She probably didn't sound all that reassuring, but then, she found that she was more nervous than she had expected to be.

The street, at first glance, looked the same as ever. It was a little after seven-thirty, the sun lowering toward the distant horizon, and the trees that lined the street cast long shadows across the blacktop. Houses had lights on in kitchens and living rooms and over front doors, but there was no one visible on the sidewalks, no one out in their yards. On a Saturday morning at least three or four people on the block would be mowing or weeding, trimming hedges, clipping trees. Now, though, the street might as well have been in a ghost town, or a movie set after filming had wrapped for the night.

Rebecca glanced anxiously at Kerry as she slowed the car, bringing them to a crawl as they neared the house. It was dark and didn't look as if anyone new had moved in since they'd left. Kerry tried to scan the cars parked along the sides of the road, in case Season was sitting in one of them watching the place. They all looked empty, and she began to think the detour was yet one more waste of time in a long day full of time wasted. As they passed the house, though, she rose up in her seat a little, staring hard at the building that had, for a brief time, contained her life on this coast. *Funny how a building can be so small, so limited, and yet hold so much inside its walls,* she thought.

And then all other thoughts vanished from her mind. Through a window, she saw something move.

"Stop!" she said, clutching hard at Rebecca's knee.

Rebecca gave a frightened squeal and

jammed on the brake, lurching the car. "What?"

"In there," Kerry said, her voice quaking. She pointed toward the house's living-room window. "Look."

The window had four panes. There were curtains over it, the same moth-eaten ones she remembered, still tied back as she'd left them her last day here. In the faint light that filtered in from the street and the setting sun, she could see figures—not just one, as she'd thought initially, but at least two or three—moving about inside. They moved in an odd, graceless fashion that somehow didn't *feel* right.

"Is it her?" Rebecca asked.

"No. I don't know who it is, but that's definitely not Season."

Rebecca started to lift her foot from the brake, but Kerry stopped her. "Wait a second. I want to get out."

Rebecca's eyes widened in fear. "But, Kerry," she argued, "you don't know who's in there, and you don't know if Season's around."

Kerry agreed, but she didn't want to admit it, even to herself. She had to know what was going on inside that house. Maybe it was something completely innocent—maybe those guys were exterminators or painters, preparing the house to be rented again.

But she didn't think so.

"If Season was hanging around," she pointed out, "she'd have seen us while we sat out here in front of the house."

Rebecca slowly pulled the car to the curb, swiveling her head in every direction to watch for sudden attack. "I'm not too sure about this. . . ."

Neither am I, Kerry thought. She knew better than to give voice to her hesitation, though. She didn't want to freak herself out, much less Rebecca, and she wanted a closer look while she had her courage worked up for it. She couldn't help wishing it were Daniel at the wheel instead of Rebecca, convinced that he'd know what to do. Or at least make her feel safer.

As soon as Rebecca killed the engine, Kerry lunged from the car. Rebecca had coasted a little past the house, so Kerry darted back toward it, hunching over in hopes that she'd be less noticeable. She knew that if whoever was inside looked out, she'd be spotted.

But the way they were moving around, it looked like they were searching for something, and she hoped all their attention was inside.

The light was fading fast. Already shadows covered the lawn, and the bushes in which Kerry had first found Daniel took on a dark, menacing appearance. Through the streaked window, she could barely see the forms she had seen just moments before, when the light was slightly better. Trying to get closer, she shoved her way through the thick bushes and pressed her face to the glass. The evening hadn't cooled off, and a film of perspiration coated her forehead, threatening to blind her, but she blinked it away.

From this spot, one could see the whole living room and into the kitchen. The kitchen had a window over the sink facing onto the tiny backyard, which meant it faced west, toward the sunset. She had loved to look through it when it was her turn to do dishes, watching birds and butterflies, and the occasional stray cat, raccoon, or opossum. Now, though, as Kerry focused on the shadowy interior, a shape crossed in front of the kitchen window, and she felt her stomach lurch.

Its form was distinctly human. It wore what seemed to be a long, dark coat, and some kind of shapeless slouch hat. But its features—unless the bad light and her own nervous system conspired to play really unpleasant tricks on her—were barely human, kind of doughy and indistinct. Her first thought was that maybe she was looking at a man who had been scarred in a horrible fire. As she watched him, though, trying to wrap her mind around what she was seeing, another came into view briefly, and he had a similar aspect. Two fire victims seemed unlikely.

Then a third appeared at the window right in front of her. Kerry screamed and ran for the car. She'd left her door open a crack, but had barely touched the seat with her butt when Rebecca peeled out like a race car driver. "What? What'd you see?" Rebecca demanded.

"It was . . . they saw me," Kerry rejoined. "They were horrible, and they saw us!"

11

Josh enjoyed hanging out with Brandy. She was lovely, for one thing, which made her easy to be around. He liked her cocoa-colored skin and athletic body and her ready smile. She was tight with Scott, of course, but that was okay—kind of relieved him of any pressure to pretend he might be interested in her as a boyfriend, since, being a girl, she definitely was not his type. But that didn't mean he didn't like to look upon beauty of whatever gender.

The day was a scorching one—each day seemed more so than the last, until Josh had to admit that a heat wave was upon them and even he, accustomed to Vegas summers, was uncomfortably warm—and she wore a knit halter top, a denim mini, and strappy sandals. Josh thought the halter was a bit much—or a bit not enough, maybe—but either way, a fashion faux pas as far as he was concerned. He'd have chosen a nice tank top, maybe, with spaghetti straps and a little more substance. The whole knit thing just smacked of eighties to him. In his baggy black jeans, Maltese Falcon movie-poster T-shirt, and spiked collar, he knew he was nobody's idea of a fashion god, but he knew what he liked.

They went into the village section of La Jolla, walking the streets of the shopping district, which centered around Prospect Street and Girard Avenue. The village retained its small resort-town air, with buildings and natural scenery reminiscent of some Mediterranean port of call. The name La Jolla, according to some, meant "the jewel," though others disputed that Chamber of Commerce–sounding translation and claimed that it was really a version of *la joya,* or "the hole," so-called because of an enormous cave that opened to the sea. Small specialty stores lined the streets, intermixed with a few nationwide chains like The Gap and Ralph Lauren. Because restaurants and bars abounded, stores stayed open late, so even though they'd taken time to watch the sun sink into the Pacific from across the grassy expanse of Ellen Browning Scripps Park, most of the shops were still occupied when they went back to browsing.

Season had never seen Brandy or Josh, so they didn't feel too exposed walking in the same general neighborhood where she had last been observed. Kerry had said Season'd eaten in the restaurant at Seaside a few times, so chances were good that she was staying in or near La Jolla.

"You think we'll recognize her if we see her?" he asked as they meandered out of what seemed like the fiftieth shoe store they'd visited. "That coffee-cup picture seems to be staying with me pretty well."

"I think he magically implanted it or something," Brandy agreed. "I don't like the idea of him messing with our heads like that."

"There isn't much about him you do like," Josh pointed out. They had agreed not to use names when they talked, because it was possible—remote, but possible—that she or some associate of hers would overhear them. Not that they thought Season had any idea who they were, but caution was the order of the day. "Smoke break," he called.

Brandy scowled at him. "Didn't you just have a smoke break?"

"That was hours ago," he argued, snaking a cigarette from the pack he kept in his hip pocket. "Or at least five shoe stores ago."

"It's like every person in La Jolla needs a new pair of shoes every day." Brandy looked at her own sandals and grimaced. "No wonder they all look so hopeful when we walk in. I really *could* use some."

Josh lit his cigarette and sucked in a lungful of smoke. He knew that Brandy was far too thrifty to buy shoes at one of these trendy shops, though. Her family had some money, according to Scott, but they had climbed to an upper-middle-class lifestyle during Brandy's lifetime, and she still knew what it was like to go without. For his part, Josh would have been happy to try life with money, having never experienced that particular sensation. Since he wouldn't wear leather, his own shoes were canvas and rubber, but the rubber was wearing awfully thin on the bottom. Soon a new semester would start up at UNLV and with it, the cost of textbooks, board, and so on. Even with financial aid, going to college was an expensive proposition.

Of course, if he'd quit smoking, he could save a hundred bucks a month. But some sacrifices were too terrible to consider.

"I'm serious," he said, trying to draw the conversation back to where he had interrupted it. "You hate him, right? You don't even buy his whole line. So why are you putting yourself through this?"

Brandy squinted at him. "You want to end up like Mace?"

"You really think that's what happened to him?"

"I don't know what else to think. If we'd heard about his death on the news, or if cops had knocked on the door and told us, maybe I'd think it was some freak accident or something. But since Da—since he came and told us about it, I figure it had to be her."

Josh blew a series of smoke rings into the still air. "Or him."

"You think he . . . ?"

"As an entrée back into our good graces? I'm just saying it's possible."

Brandy shook her head. "Anything's possible, Josh. But is it likely? Or have you just watched too many conspiracy movies?"

"He's just one guy, so it's not exactly a conspiracy," Josh observed. "And yeah, maybe I've read a lot of noir crime stories with some pretty convoluted plots. But hey, if those writers could think those stories up, then regular people can come up with some twisted ideas too. And to hear him talk, it sounds like he's loaded with twisted ideas."

"What, now you're saying you don't believe any of this?" Brandy asked.

Josh dropped his cigarette butt to the sidewalk and ground it under his shoe. "I didn't say that," he countered. As much as he liked being with Brandy, sometimes talking to her was exhausting. She had a tendency to question and analyze and interpret even the most casual comments. "At first I thought somebody scared his momma with an Anne Rice novel when he was *in utero*, but there's obviously more to him than there is to us. We've all seen that. I'm only saying it doesn't hurt to keep an open mind, you know? Cooperate with him, but keep an eye on him at the same time. Just in case."

Now Brandy nodded her agreement. "You know I've never liked him or trusted him. I'm trying to because if he's right, then our lives might depend on him. Probably they do. But if he's pulling some kind of fast one, I want to be ready to put some major distance between me and him in a heartbeat. And I don't want anybody getting in my way. You know what they say about what you have to do when you're hiking with a friend and a bear charges you?"

Josh spread his arms, indicating his slight frame and his utter lack of a tan. "Not exactly Mr. Outdoors here."

"You don't have to be able to outrun the bear," Brandy elaborated. "As long as you can outrun your friend."

Josh laughed, surprised to hear a sentiment like that coming from Brandy. He guessed he shouldn't have been. *Girl has a pragmatic streak as wide as the Grand Canyon,* he thought. It seemed to put her at odds, sometimes, with her hopelessly idealistic boyfriend Scott, to whom every newspaper or news broadcast held fresh outrage.

"What's the matter with this state?" Scott had exploded at breakfast that morning. "California drinks half the bottled water consumed in the country. But only sixteen percent of the bottles are recycled! A billion plastic water bottles a year go into landfill."

Brandy had calmed him down, as somehow she seemed supremely able to do, but Josh had felt a little sorry for Daniel, having to go out hunting with Scott today. He was sure to return to the water-bottle crisis several times during the search.

"So you're of the 'keep your friends close and your enemies closer' school?" Josh asked.

"Pretty much," Brandy replied. "I'm not saying he's our enemy. So far he hasn't done anything to hurt us, unless he really is responsible for Mace somehow. And this Sea—the other one," she caught herself, "sounds like a real piece of work. So I'm willing to give him the benefit of the doubt, at least until he proves otherwise."

Josh shrugged. "Works for me," he said. "Let's check out the next shoe store."

The next store, in fact, was a children's clothing store—children's clothing for millionaires, Brandy pointed out when she saw the price tags—and they only stayed a moment, long enough to ascertain that Season was not picking up a new bib or a thousand-dollar velvet toddler's dress. After that came an art gallery specializing, it seemed, in pieces that made no sense at all to Josh's untrained eye, and then an Oriental rug shop. *Then* a shoe store.

But it wasn't until they had reached a woman's boutique with a cutesy name that Josh forgot as soon as they had passed beneath the sign, that they saw her. Josh was eyeing the salesman, who wore bleached-out jeans and a tight, striped shirt, its sleeves rolled back over muscular forearms, when he felt Brandy's fingers dig into the flesh of his upper arm.

He looked at her, and she ticked her eyes toward the other side of the store. An attractive blonde woman held up a purple silk shirt in front of herself and examined the look in a mirror.

"Is that her?" Josh whispered. He couldn't be sure he had actually made any sound at all. His heart was suddenly pounding as if a marching-band drummer straddled his back.

But when Brandy said, "It's her," he could hear that. Brandy still hadn't let go of his arm, and it hurt when she forcibly turned him around and marched him from the shop.

"What are you doing?" he asked as soon as they hit the sidewalk. "She's inside."

"Right. You see a back door? I didn't. She's not sneaking out. But we need to get *him* down here—nothing we can do by ourselves."

"Gotcha," Josh agreed. He fumbled his cell phone from his pocket.

"Not here," Brandy hissed. She grabbed him again and tugged him down a couple of store-fronts. "We don't want her to see us and know something's up. You heard what he said—she's too strong unless he has surprise on his side. If he can take her when she's walking out of a store, unsuspecting, he might have a chance. If she sees some freaked-out Goth boy screaming into his cell phone, she'll be on her guard."

"He'll have to be close by," Josh pointed out. He gestured with the phone, which was still undialed, to where Season was walking out of the store, emptyhanded, a small purse dangling on a long strap from her shoulder. *Leather, too,* he thought. *I hate her.*

"We'll just follow her," Brandy said. "Keep tabs on her."

But even that simple plan wouldn't work quite so easily since, apparently done with her shopping, Season approached a BMW Z4 convertible parked at one of the angled spaces by the curb, underneath a streetlight. "Oh, no," Josh moaned. "She's driving."

Street parking being a precious commodity in La Jolla, especially in summer, their own wheels were in a parking garage beneath an office building, more than a block away. "I'll go for the car," Brandy said urgently. "You call him, and keep her in sight."

She took off running without waiting for an answer. As he watched her disappearing form, Josh had no doubt she was, in fact, faster than the bear. Or at least faster than him.

He punched up Daniel's number and hit send. A moment later, the now-familiar voice came on the line. "Yes."

"Sh-she's here," Josh stammered. "In La Jolla. The village. On Girard. She just came out of a store and got into a car, a silver BMW."

"I'm on my way," Daniel said. "Keep watching her. Let me know where she goes."

"One problem. I'm on foot. Brandy's gone to get the car."

The silver BMW waited for a couple of cars to pass and then began to back carefully from its parking space. Josh started walking quickly toward it, torn between not wanting to attract attention and not wanting to let Season escape his sight.

"Do you know how to hotwire a car?" Daniel asked him. The witch sounded breathless, and Josh figured he was already running to his own wheels.

"Only in theory," Josh said. "I've seen it done in movies. Not in real life."

"Never mind, then. Just keep an eye on her, any way you can."

"I'm trying." Josh broke into a run then, because Season had cleared the parking space and begun driving up Girard, away from Prospect Street and the ocean. There was traffic, though, and she wasn't going very fast. When he reached an intersection, he hurtled into it without looking, and a car trying to cross the wide expanse of Girard squealed its tires, stopping for him. "She's driving," he panted into the phone. "I don't know how long I can keep up."

"Don't lose her!" Daniel ordered. Josh could hear the roar of his engine over the phone. "Can you get the license number?"

Then he heard Scott's voice. "Is Brandy there? Is she all right?"

"Tell him she's fine," Josh replied, huffing. "And I can see B523 . . . can't make out the rest. . . ." Ahead of him the BMW started to accelerate up a long, traffic-free stretch of road. He broke into a sprint, awkwardly trying to hold the phone to his ear as he ran. Every few paces he craned his neck to see if—*please, please!*—Brandy was drawing up behind him.

"Do you still see her?" Daniel demanded urgently.

Josh ran with everything he had, but the BMW reached the intersection. Her brake lights flashed once, and she made a right turn, immediately vanishing behind the building on the corner. "Nooo!" Josh yelled.

"What?" Daniel wanted to know.

Josh kept up his pace, swallowing sidewalk with every step. But the corner was still too far away—more than a city block, on the other side of a supermarket parking lot. He'd never make it. She would be long out of sight before he could reach it.

"She turned a corner," he breathed into the phone. Finally he stopped running. "I lost her."

"Are you sure?" Daniel asked.

Josh did a quick scan. He could cut through the supermarket's lot. If she'd been stuck at the next light, where Fay Street crossed Pearl Street, he might still get a glimpse of her at that intersection. "There's one more thing I can try," he said, though he wasn't sure how he was going to get his legs to take another step.

"Do it!"

Josh was about to obey when a horn honked on the street beside him. Brandy was finally there in Scott's RAV4. She popped open the passenger door and he forced himself to hurry the four steps to the car. "Up to the corner," he managed, folding in on himself from the ache in his chest and lungs, trying to ignore the sweat that ran in rivers down his sides and soaked his back. "Turn right."

Brandy floored it, racing up the street, braking just enough not to lose control as the car screamed around the corner. The car's rear end fishtailed a little, but the tires bit and held on to the road. Josh put his left hand on the dash in front of him and searched Pearl Street.

No BMW in sight. Brandy drove the length of the street, and he watched every parking lot, every side street. In a few moments they were dipping down toward the ocean. "Which way?" she asked.

Josh could only shake his head.

"We're almost there," Daniel's voice said. Josh had forgotten the phone, still clutched in his right fist. "Do you have her?"

"She's gone," Josh admitted. "We can't see her at all."

"Keep cruising," Daniel said. "Maybe you'll pick her up again. Did she know you were onto her?"

Only if she looked in her mirror and saw a maniac running up the sidewalk, Josh thought. He felt defeated, broken. "I don't know."

Brandy took the road down toward the water. It wound between luxury apartments and condominiums, then, on the ocean side, a few sprawling homes and then nothing but cliffs and coast.

"Where are you?" Daniel asked after another few minutes. "We're at Girard and Pearl."

"She went right there," Josh told him. "We went toward the water."

"We'll turn up La Jolla Boulevard, then," Daniel reported. "Maybe she's heading toward Pacific Beach."

"I'm sorry, Daniel. I really did try."

There was a long moment of silence from the other end, and Josh wasn't sure if Daniel had even heard him. But then he answered. "It's okay, Josh. You guys found her. We can do it again."

12

Scott Banner was pretty sure he was going to die.

Daniel had magical powers or whatever, so he could probably survive the collision of the rented (or stolen, he wasn't entirely sure which) Ford Taurus with any of the half-dozen vehicles it had almost smashed into, not to mention lane dividers and walls, as Daniel piloted it at breakneck speeds from Del Mar to La Jolla. But any of those near misses could have spelled instant extinction for Scott, who held onto his seat belt's shoulder strap for dear life on each occasion.

Fortunately Daniel seemed to have an inordinately sure hand with the wheel, and his touch with the brake—though used sparingly— was also confident and precise. Of course, he drove one-handed, with his cell phone glued to his ear by the other, which made the whole experience that much more nerve-racking. They raced down the coast road (ocean to their right, lagoons to their left), then up the hill past Torrey Pines State Reserve, along the cliffs between the Scripps Institute and the University of California at San Diego, of which the campus looked lovely, if a bit blurry, finally speeding down the hill into La Jolla proper. Fortunately they had already been headed in that general direction, having stopped at one of the beaches to see if Season was there. If they'd been far from the car, or going the other way, Scott wouldn't have wanted to see what shortcuts Daniel might have made to save time.

A few minutes after reaching La Jolla, they rendezvoused with Brandy and Josh in the parking lot of a chain drugstore. Josh still looked out of breath, his pale, sunken cheeks rosy with the effort he'd put into the chase. Scott climbed gratefully from the car and enveloped Brandy in a hug, pulling her close and sniffing the vaguely vanilla-like scent of whatever she used on her thick, luxuriant hair.

"Are you okay?" he asked. "Did she see you?"

Brandy disengaged, shaking her head. When she answered him, her usual antagonism toward Daniel had vanished. "She might have seen Josh. I'm sure she didn't see me—if we'd been close enough for that, we'd still be on her tail. Woman can move."

"How did you find her?"

"We just walked into a dress store and there she was, looking just like she did in that coffee cup," Brandy announced.

"Did you . . . like, cement that image in our heads somehow?" Josh inquired of Daniel. "Because when we saw her, both of us were, like, pow, that's her."

"When I conjured it there was a retention spell involved," Daniel admitted. He didn't sound reluctant or embarrassed about it, Scott noted. Just as if it had been something so mundane he'd forgotten to mention it. *A retention spell. When I conjured it. Like I'd say, "I flipped on the light switch."*

Of course, Scott realized, *to me it is basically magic how the electricity gets from the river, or the coal plant, or whatever, to the light socket. So I guess to him it's just another kind of science.*

Maybe something anyone can do with the right kind of calculator and test tubes. To the liberal-arts undergrad, all science is magic.

Daniel turned to Josh. "Can you show me where she was standing?"

Josh pointed in the general direction. "Over there," he replied. "On Girard."

"No," Daniel corrected. "I mean, precisely. Can you show me a spot where you know, with absolute certainty, her feet touched the ground?"

"I can," Brandy volunteered. "In the store. Her bag was bumping into a top I thought looked really cute. Unless they've rearranged the display in the last thirty minutes, I can show it to you."

"Let's go," Daniel said.

Parking being the losing proposition that it was, they left the cars in the drugstore lot—risking tickets or towing, Scott noted, because the lot had FOR CUSTOMERS ONLY signs posted in huge red letters—and walked back to the boutique. On the way Daniel called Kerry's phone and told her to meet them back at the drugstore's parking lot.

In the store the salesman looked at them

expectantly when they walked in, but Josh waved and said, "We're only looking," and the guy went behind the counter and sat on a stool with a glum sigh.

Brandy pointed out to Daniel exactly where the witch had been standing when they'd seen her. "Right here," she said. Turning to Scott, she fingered a shimmery green blouse and added, "And if you want to pick up an early birthday present, check this out."

But Scott couldn't even get close enough to see the price tag. Daniel squatted down on the ground and touched his fingers to the floor. Scott was reminded of trackers in Western movies, feeling for the oncoming thunder of a buffalo herd. Then Daniel stood and sniffed the air. After a few moments of that, he froze, standing utterly still, eyes closed, lips parted slightly. It was, Scott believed, exceedingly strange behavior. But he presumed that it meant something. Either that or Daniel was a gifted con man, pulling a fast one on them by acting out the oddest routine he could come up with.

While Daniel performed his awkward gyrations, Brandy took Scott's hand and squeezed. "I guess we did okay," she said softly. "I mean, I wish we hadn't lost her. But at least we spotted her once, right?"

"You sound like a convert," he responded. Secretly he was glad. He'd believed in Daniel almost from the beginning—or, more precisely, he'd believed in Kerry's judgment, and if she wanted Daniel around, that was good enough for him. Brandy had doubted him with such rabid certainty that it had put Scott in an uncomfortable position. If she was coming around, that would make his life easier.

"I wouldn't go that far," she hedged. "But maybe I'm mellowing about it. A little. Now that I know Season Howe is real, I guess."

"Nothing wrong with that," Scott said, hoping he sounded neutral but encouraging.

Without a word to the rest of them, Daniel stalked outside, nose in the air as if he were following a scent. The sales clerk watched them go, confusion written all over his face. Josh tossed him a shrug and a smile, and then trailed after Daniel.

On the sidewalk, Brandy squeezed Scott's hand again and nodded toward Daniel, who came to a stop underneath a streetlight. "He's following her path exactly," she reported. "Walking exactly where she did."

"Weird," Scott uttered. He'd been with Daniel the whole time, so he knew the man couldn't possibly have seen Season's moves. Which meant that somehow, even after this long, he was able to sense where she'd been.

"Uh-huh," Brandy agreed. "Like I said, the realer this gets, the more I'm into it."

"You never said that," Scott reminded her. "At least, not to me."

"Maybe not. But I meant it."

Kerry and Rebecca hadn't been far from La Jolla, still working south through Pacific Beach, when Kerry's phone trilled like an agitated bird. She answered it and heard Daniel's voice, sounding strained and urgent. "Are you all right?"

"Fine. What's up?"

He didn't answer the question, but instead gave her instructions to meet the rest of the group at a drugstore's parking lot. Kerry relayed the message to Rebecca, who turned the car around—avoiding the street they'd raced away from, not so long before—and drove back up to La Jolla. When they got there, they found the RAV4 and the Taurus parked side by side, but saw no sign of the gang. Kerry and Rebecca stood by Rebecca's car, waiting, making uncomfortable small talk. Both of them were still freaked by what Kerry had seen in their old house—Kerry by the sight itself, and Rebecca by Kerry's reaction to it. Kerry thought about the conversation they'd had when she'd jumped back into the car.

"You look like you're being chased by ghosts," Rebecca had said to her.

"I don't know what they were," Kerry had admitted, trying to bring her voice under control. "'Ghosts' is probably as good a word as any."

"You're kidding," Rebecca had said. She had stared at Kerry for so long, Kerry worried they'd run off the road.

"Watch where you're going," Kerry had ordered. "I'd like to live long enough to ask Daniel what those guys were."

"You think they were, like, Season's familiars or something?"

"I thought a familiar was like a black cat. Anyway he hasn't said anything about her having any. But maybe."

Rebecca had offered a couple more suggestions, but Kerry found she wasn't interested in hearing the theories of someone who—while truly wanting to help—could not possibly have any idea what they were up against. Her monosyllabic answers discouraged Rebecca, who eventually stopped trying to talk to Kerry. Then the phone had gone off. And here they were; Kerry still lost in questions she couldn't answer, Rebecca keeping her distance.

As they waited in the parking lot, though, Kerry understood what had happened, and how she'd shut Rebecca out, who was just about the most well-intentioned person she'd ever known. "Hey," she said apologetically, "I didn't mean to be a shrew or anything. I was just, you know, kind of preoccupied."

Rebecca smiled, her whole face seeming to brighten, though in the harsh light of day it was a little hard to tell. "That's okay," she said. "Perfectly understandable, considering . . . you know. Whatever you saw."

"That's the big question, isn't it?"

Rebecca reached for Kerry as if to give her a hug, but Kerry didn't feel quite that sisterly yet. Rebecca caught the vibe, though, and just rubbed Kerry's shoulder instead. "One thing I do want to say, though, is how impressed I was."

"Impressed?" *Color me confused*, Kerry thought. *Maybe I set a new land-speed record when I ran away from the house.*

"The way you walked right up to the window, even though you'd seen someone inside," Rebecca explained. "I couldn't have done that. I just about left a puddle in my car seat, waiting for you. I don't think I've ever seen something so brave."

Kerry was complimented to hear her say that, but puzzled by the sentiment. "All I did was check it out," she said. "Nothing special about that."

"You don't think so," Rebecca countered, "because you're a brave person. So it doesn't seem like much."

Kerry felt herself blushing now, heat rising from her chest, engulfing her neck and face. In spite of her pale complexion, she didn't blush often, but once she did, her body committed to it. She turned away from Rebecca, just in time to see Daniel and the others walking from the corner of Girard Avenue and Pearl Street. Daniel led the way, his gait purposeful. Kerry was surprised to feel a small thrill at the sight of him, more or less encompassing the same region as the blush she'd experienced moments before.

When he reached the parking lot, he looked around, and she thought—or hoped—that meant he was seeking her out. His face gave a spark of recognition when he saw her, she believed—a lift of the jaw, a twitch of a smile, a brightening of the eyes. It might have been a trick of the light.

But maybe not.

"You're okay?" he asked when he reached her, holding out his hand for hers.

"Why wouldn't I be?" She liked the pressure of his hand grasping hers, engulfing it with warmth and concern.

But after a moment Daniel released her hand and glanced up and down the street. The others caught up to them as he was doing so. "She was here," he said. "You lost her here, on Pearl, right?" This was directed to Josh, who nodded morosely.

"Right."

"She was here?" Kerry asked. "Season?"

"That's right," Brandy said. "Josh and I saw her, but we lost her."

Daniel's gaze darted about again, and Kerry realized he was as alert as a cat in an aviary, ready for Season to return to try something, or just to pass this way again. "I can almost sense her," he explained. "It's like an aftertaste, kind of metallic somehow. It happens when I get close to her."

"Even when you're running from her?" Josh asked. "Like the other night, with Kerry?"

Daniel nodded. "It's how I knew she was in the restaurant."

The admission startled Kerry, though it didn't seem like anyone else realized its import. If he hadn't known Season would be at the restaurant, then he'd have had no reason to go there.

Unless he'd gone to see Kerry.

She couldn't say, at that moment, exactly how she felt about that possibility.

But she thought she liked it.

13

Somehow the seating arrangements for the cars going back to Imperial Beach were shuffled, and Kerry wound up riding with Daniel. Not that she was complaining. In fact, all other considerations aside, she still wanted to ask him about what she had seen in the house. Her initial fear was that he might want to drive by and check it out for himself, but he put that to rest immediately.

"They're simulacra," he said quite matter-of-factly, when she described them.

"They're what?"

"Simulacra. Not really human, but human in structure. They can pass for human, if no one looks too closely."

"Are they . . . do they work for her?" Kerry asked nervously. "For Season?"

Daniel laughed softly as he tooled down the freeway in the dark. "No. No, they work for us."

Shocked, Kerry wasn't sure what to say to that. *Seems like something you should have mentioned,* she thought. But the words wouldn't come out of her mouth.

"Well, for my mother, to be more exact," he went on. "It's a little stunt of hers."

"Your mother?" Kerry realized she sounded stupid parroting what she had just heard, and she had a vague memory of Brandy saying the same words, with very nearly the same surprised tone, many nights before. But the words slipped out of her mouth before she could rein them in.

"Mother Blessing," he confirmed. "That's what everyone calls her. Myself included."

"Seems a little formal," Kerry suggested. "For someone you've known for three hundred years."

"Maybe," Daniel agreed. "But then, she's not much like other mothers. Or at least that's the impression I get, having only had the one."

Kerry felt herself reddening for the second time tonight. "I'm sorry," she said. "I guess I . . .

when you told the story about Slocumb, you said your mother had survived. I didn't realize you meant she was still alive."

"Still alive," he confirmed, glancing out the rear window and changing lanes to the right. "Not as well as she used to be, I'm afraid. Witches do age, just more slowly than most."

"And she's still hunting for Season?" Kerry pressed.

"She does what she can."

Daniel moved farther right, exiting the freeway. A couple of minutes to the apartment, and their brief time alone would be over. She found the prospect sad. But then she mentally chastised herself, knowing she shouldn't even be thinking like that. There was nothing between her and Daniel, and there couldn't ever be. He was not just an older man than her, he was older than her great-grandparents would have been if they were still alive. Which, of course, they weren't, because, hey, *old*. She didn't see that when she looked at him. He looked like a man in his late twenties, perhaps, now that he was fully healed. Early thirties, maybe.

And in addition to being easy to look at, he

was charming and fascinating. From time to time she thought him humorless, but then his dry wit would show through, and she'd realize that it was simply that he was preoccupied and that his quest was more important to him than the ability to crack jokes. She could honestly say that she had never known anyone quite like him.

"These simulacra you saw," Daniel said, after they'd reached the surface street. "Mother Blessing didn't tell me she was sending them, but from your description I'm positive that's what they were. They were doubtlessly searching the house for signs of Season."

"But that was our house, not hers."

"Right," Daniel agreed. "And by now she has surely found it and gone inside looking for similar signs of me. In doing so, she might have left behind an energy signature the simulacra could pick up on."

"But you're just speculating, right?"

"Informed speculation, let's say. If Season had developed the ability to manifest and control simulacra, I think I'd know about it."

"Can she just come up with new powers like that?"

Daniel laughed again. "You can, in fact,

teach an old dog new tricks," he said. "Or an old witch, at any rate. But creating simulacra really is one of Mother Blessing's trademarks. So chances are good they were hers. Even so, they can be dangerous, so it's good you kept your distance."

"I thought they were on our side," Kerry said.

"They are. But they're not truly human, and their powers of reasoning are essentially nonexistent. They take orders, that's all. If you should see any again, I'd recommend you keep well away from them."

"I'll do my best," Kerry promised. Their apartment building loomed before them in the night. "I'd like to know more about her. Your mother, I mean," Kerry heard herself saying, though the thought had never before crossed her mind.

"I told you I'd let you read some of my notebooks," Daniel reminded her. "Why not start tonight?"

I knew the weather was changing as soon as I walked outside and felt the north wind on my face, cold and crisp as a winter's day. The trapper's cabin was in a clearing with a creek running behind it, and ponderosa pines as far as I could see in front. Through the trees I could just see a snow-capped mountain peak. I shouldered my rifle and began the day's hunt.

She had been here, this much I knew. Not so long ago. The cabin I had slept in the night before had been inhabited by her, within the past week. I could still smell her on the walls, the floors, the scant furnishings. Not long ago she had slept in that place, though not for the last few nights. The night before I had rested with eyes half open and no fire, just in case she returned. But she did not.

Kerry put the dense leather book down on her bed. Daniel had handed her two of them, both wrapped with leather thongs to hold them closed, both heavier than modern books, by almost double. The journals were about six by nine inches, she figured, and held a hundred or so leaves of thick paper on which Daniel had written in an ink that had turned the color of rust. His handwriting was meticulous, and even on the yellowed, flaking pages she found it easy to read. "I don't know what years these cover," he said. "I never have bothered to date the outsides. But I'm sure you'll find one just as impenetrable as the next." She took the volumes, surprised by their unexpected weight, and her fingers had brushed his as she did. He smiled and left her alone in the room. Rebecca was out with Brandy and Scott, talking over the day's events, but Kerry had retired early, anxious to start on Daniel's journals.

> *During the few minutes that I slept soundly during the night, horrifying nightmares had been my reward. This only confirmed my belief that Season Howe had found refuge under this same roof— even the air inside had been twisted and distorted by contact with her, by the evil miasma she leaves behind everywhere she passes. My dreams had been full of death: carcasses missing their heads, blood flowing freely from their necks; disemboweled men with innards yanked out as if by butcher's hooks, streaming from their bellies; worms and vermin crawling about in the midst of*

all this carnage. These were not, need I say, normal dreams for me, but were surely caused by her proximity.

I knew, therefore, that she was not far away. But the wind from the north meant two things to me. One, by the time the sun set, the day would be far colder than it was now, and two, a stiff wind would scour her tracks, making it even harder to find her. I had come close, but missed her by days. Now I had to follow a trail that was already growing cold, and I had to do so before weather made the task impossible.

At first I had an easy enough go of it. The same tracks that had led me to the cabin were still visible to me, though most of them would not be to a normal, human tracker. Season had been traveling fast, heedless of such things as broken twigs on the forest floor, or bits of fabric, or long blonde hair caught on limbs. And less visible to others were what I have taken to calling her miasmic tracks, the traces of evil that glow in her wake with a foul green tinge. The color of sickness.

I was right where the weather was concerned. By midmorning the air had turned frigid, and the wind bit at my cheeks and hands like a whip. Shortly after noon, a time I marked only by removing a lump of hardtack from my sack and chewing it as I walked, the first snow flurried around me.

My other fear was borne out as well. The ever more powerful winds scattered leaves where her feet might have made impressions, picked up and hurled away those stray hairs and threads, and generally slowed my progress. I began to hope some other trapper's cabin would present itself by dark, or the night would be unpleasant indeed.

To my surprise, though, when I crested a low hill I saw before me a valley containing a small settlement. A mining community; even from the hillside I could see headframes on the opposite slope. A score of buildings, mostly of wood, huddled around one sad-looking, rutted wagon road. The sun had become a cold, flat disk that looked impossibly distant, and even if

Season's tracks had not led me this way I would have sought refuge in the town for the night. As it was, dark had fallen by the time I reached it.

But when I approached the buildings on the road, I noticed something I had not from above while the sun yet shone. Though it was past dusk, there were no lights in any of them, no flicker of candle or lantern or fireplace glowing through windows. The same wind I had battled all day whistled between the cold, stark buildings. Somewhere a shutter banged; that and the wind were the only sounds besides that of my own feet, trudging on hard-packed earth.

Seeing no one, hearing no other noise, I felt a chill to my core. I should call out, I knew, to see if anyone was about. But what if she was here? Would making my own presence known put me at her mercy? I feared that it might, and decided to investigate at a more cautious pace. I started with the nearest house, and rapped upon the door.

Hearing nothing from within, I

opened it. Instantly the reek of death assailed me. Bracing myself I went farther into the house's cold bowels, only to find, in the kitchen, the remains of three people. I could not be certain, but it looked like a man, a woman, and their daughter, a girl of perhaps twelve or thirteen. Fat, lazy flies sated themselves on pools of blood. Gagging, I hurried away from the grisly scene.

But similar sights greeted me in the next house and the next. The town had been massacred—one house, one family, at a time. I was put in mind of Slocumb, although in that instance, of course, the town's death had come all at once in a horrible swirl of destruction, according to the stories Mother Blessing tells. I felt sure that the cause was the same; that the tragedy that had struck this town, whatever it was called, wore the name of Season Howe.

Finally I went into a house and heard, or thought I heard, the scuttling sounds of inhabitants from somewhere in the back. Rats, I told myself, or some other vermin, no doubt feasting on the dead. I readied my rifle and kicked open the door behind which I had heard the noises.

It was no rat, though, or other creature of field and fen. It was a man, wild-eyed and unshaven, staring at me from behind a flintlock pistol of his own, and from behind a mask of madness. His clothes were tattered and covered in blood, but it took me a moment to see the source of the blood. In the corner behind him were the ravaged remains of three other people. My first instinct was that I had caught him in the act of despoiling the remains, possibly even cannibalizing them. But upon regarding him further, his stance appeared defensive, as if he were simply trying to protect them. The antique firearm trained on me enhanced this impression.

"Rest easy, friend," I said. "I am here to help if I can."

When he replied, the madness that flitted across his face came through in his voice as well, high-pitched and anxious. "Nothing to be done. Nothing anyone can do. Go 'way."

"How did this happen?" I asked. "Who did all this?"

He twitched the gun at me. "Go 'way, while you can. Sickness here, sickness spreads."

"I might be able to do something," I said. I knew not what I could truly do to help, but my abilities were beyond those of others, so I prayed that perhaps there was still hope for someone in this forsaken place.

"Too late, way too late," the man said. He giggled when he said it, a sound so girlish it seemed unnatural coming from such a grizzled old man.

"Was there a witch here?" I demanded. "A woman with blond hair and smooth features hiding the evil beneath?"

"She was here, she was here," the man answered. "Too late, though. Everyone's too late. Months too late. Years. Too, too, too."

"She did this?" I was sure I knew the answer. This looked like Season's handiwork, to me. "She killed everyone?"

"Too late, too late," the man said again. His face twitched, and I worried that if his finger tightened on the trigger of that weapon, I would be in sorry shape as well.

Sensing that I would get no useful answers from this tragic soul, I shouldered my own weapon again. "I am sorry to have disturbed you, sir," I told him. "I shall find myself someplace in town to sleep tonight, and then tomorrow I will be on my way. If there is anything I can do to help you, just ask."

The man let out a plaintive mewl then, like a kitten begging for milk. He spoke not, though, made no intelligible request of me, which I would gladly have done my best to fulfill. So I took my leave, shaking my head sadly at the wretched state to which he had fallen, which had, indeed, beset this entire town. If he was the sole survivor, as seemed to be the case, then the town was tragic indeed.

I had barely reached the front door of his house when I heard his ancient weapon discharge. I turned and rushed back into the room in which I had left him. He was still there, but there was no life in him. A new hole had appeared in his forehead, and a spray of blood and bone decorated the horrific scene behind him. The gun was still clutched in his right hand, a thin plume of smoke issuing from its barrel.

I write this in a room of the town's boardinghouse, denoted by a sign beside the door. Downstairs are more dead, but this room I found empty and clean. If there is sickness here, it will affect me not at all. Tomorrow I will perform a cleansing spell to make doubly sure of that and to ease the way for whatever visitor comes here next. But I am not certain that it will do any good. Despite what the man told me—and his madness, I feel sure, makes all of his words suspect—this looks to me like yet another town that has fallen prey to Season's hatred.

I mourn for this nameless town and its people. And I renew my vow to find her, to destroy her, in the name of the people of Slocumb, and now of this place and of any *others who have crossed her path.*

My candle gutters, my eyes grow heavy. Even in the face of terrible tragedy, sleep makes its demands.

I remain, Daniel Blessing. Fifteenth of September, 1854.

Kerry closed the book. She hadn't expected to have read this long—Rebecca had come in, wished her good night, and gone to sleep, while Kerry sat turning pages by the light of a bedside lamp. But then, she hadn't expected the story to take on such a horrific aspect. She had thought it would be a record like most days she'd spent with Daniel—looking for Season, not finding her, getting up and doing it again.

Having read it, though, she felt like she had a more visceral understanding of Daniel's quest, of the urgency of it. *If "urgency" can be applied to an effort that's been ongoing for hundreds of years,* Kerry thought. But who knew what terrors Season had cooked up in that time, if this sort of thing was a habit with her?

Kerry remembered the nightmares she'd been having, in the weeks before Daniel had appeared in their yard—nightmares that had ended at that time, and about which she'd forgotten until reading about the ones that Daniel had in Season's proximity. Could there be some connection to hers? She didn't know how that could be, though. Anyway, they hadn't recurred, even though there was more in her life that might lead to bad dreams now. She felt tired, but she wasn't sure how she'd sleep that night. Determined to try, though, she switched off her light, put her head down on the pillow, and closed her eyes.

14

"I'm going to try to pick up Season's trail where we lost it last night," Daniel announced the next morning. Scott and Brandy hadn't shown themselves yet, but the rest of them were up, eating breakfast, and sipping tea or the coffee that Daniel had brewed.

Having read the part of his journal that she had, Kerry understood that the effort wouldn't necessarily be as hopeless as it sounded. "I'll go with."

Daniel shook his head. "It's not safe."

"Safe?" Kerry echoed, incredulous. "With Season out there somewhere, what does safe even mean? Is there such a concept?"

"I wouldn't argue with the Bulldog if I were you," Rebecca warned Daniel. "She's a tough one."

"I know that," Daniel agreed with a hint of a smile. "Believe me, one doesn't have to know Kerry long to figure that out."

"So?" Kerry pressed, oddly pleased to hear Daniel acknowledge a personality trait she wasn't always so fond of. "There's some forward momentum here, and I want to be along in case anything happens."

"When I find her, I don't want you close by," Daniel protested. "Any of you. The next time we meet it's going to be bad, and I don't want to have to worry about you getting hurt."

"Is that why you didn't take her at the restaurant that night?" Josh wondered. "Because you didn't want Kerry or Mace to get hurt?"

"That, and I wasn't fully recovered from our previous encounter," Daniel admitted. "I am now. And there's Mace to hold her accountable for, on top of everything else she's done."

"I didn't know Mace meant that much to you," Brandy put in sleepily. She shuffled in from her room, rubbing her eyes, a bathrobe tied with a sash over her silk pj's. "You sure didn't show it when he was alive."

"Brandy—," Kerry began, but Daniel cut her off.

"You're right, Brandy," he said. "Mace was no fan of mine, and I probably didn't do enough to win him over. I misread him or I would never have let him try to drive off alone. But he was one of you, and I consider myself responsible for the lot of you, in some ways."

"We can take care of ourselves," Josh countered, sounding defiant.

"You could, before I came along. Now, not so much."

"We've been over this before," Kerry said, casting a sharp look Brandy's way. "Rehashing it now doesn't do us any good."

Brandy stifled a yawn. "Yeah, I know. Sorry." She didn't sound much like she meant it, but Kerry figured that was as good as it would get.

"So when do we leave?" she asked Daniel.

He put his cup into the sink with a clatter and ran hot water over it for a moment. "No time like the present," he said. "Let's go."

Back to La Jolla again. Again Daniel parked near the intersection of Girard and Pearl, which was the last place Josh had definitely seen Season. The morning sun was bright, the skies blue and cloudless, and she could smell the slightest trace of sea air on the gentle breeze, reminding her how much she missed her daily communion with the ocean. Daniel got out of the Taurus and walked to the corner, waited a moment for traffic to clear, and then went out into the street. Glancing both ways to make sure it was safe, he squatted down and touched the pavement with his right hand. He shook his head, moved to a spot farther toward the edge of the lane, and repeated the same process. This time Kerry saw a smile curl the edges of his mouth. He jogged back to the safety of the sidewalk as the next wave of cars came toward the corner.

"She was here," he confirmed. "She came this way."

"That's what Josh said, right?"

"And I didn't doubt him," Daniel explained. "But Season can be trickier than most people think. I needed to know for myself."

"Okay," Kerry said. "So now what?"

"Now we follow." He began walking down

Pearl, eyeing the street as if he could see her trail. Maybe he could—maybe that green-tinted track Daniel had followed in the journal still existed.

"On foot?" she asked, surprised. Season had been driving a BMW, according to Josh and Brandy. Following on foot seemed pointless.

"It's much harder to track from a moving vehicle," Daniel told her. "But once we have an idea of what direction she's heading, I may ask you to drive ahead, just so the car is never too far from us."

Kerry shrugged and watched him move on, his face turned toward the street, ignoring the curious looks of people in passing vehicles. That image summed him up, she believed, the intrepid seeker, carrying on his quest no matter what the obstacles, or the opinions, of others might be. She couldn't decide if it made him a humorous figure or a tragic one . . . or simply heroic. *Probably a combination of all three. But considering what Season's done, weighted toward heroic.* She hurried to catch up with him, mindful that she might be sent back for the car at any moment.

· · ·

Kerry Profitt's diary, August 25

This is when the world stopped making sense:

Daniel and I had spent the morning tracking Season, and making good progress. At least according to Daniel. As far as I could tell, he was just following one random street after another, but he insisted that her car had driven on all these streets. Through Bird Rock and into Pacific Beach we went, me running for the car from time to time, and him even getting into it once in awhile, when it looked like she was going in a straight line for a long stretch.

But the day wore on and even he gets hungry sometimes, so we stopped for a pizza at a place on Turquoise Street. We're waiting for the food, sipping our drinks, tired and hungry. And his hand is resting on the table. It's just a hand, tan and muscular, I guess, if a hand can be muscular, with long, lean fingers. Well-shaped, I suppose you'd call it, if you called it anything at all. Little scars here and there, and I know from experience that it's a working man's hand, not an indoors hand. Callused and rough sometimes.

So out of nowhere—and I mean that literally, because as surprised as he was, I think I was even more so—I took his hand in mine. Both of mine, actually. Picked it up off the table and held it, kind of caressing it. He closed his fingers around my hand, but there was shock in his eyes, and a kind of hesitant half smile on his lips.

"I know I have a long way to go in the journals," I said. "But are there many women in there? Besides Season, I mean. You've lived so long, and you're so wonderful and handsome, there must have been some in your past. You never talk about them, though."

Daniel sighed and nodded. "There have been some," he said. "Not so many. And fewer who really meant anything."

"Why?" I felt like someone peeking through her fingers at the scariest part of a horror movie, not wanting to see but wanting to at the same time. Was I sure I needed to hear this?

"Ask again later," quoth the 8-ball.

But he answered me anyway. "It's hard. I'm always on the move, always on the hunt. If I did fall in love with someone, would that slow me down? Probably. Would it give Season an edge she could use against me? Certainly. And then there's the other problem. . . ."

"What problem?"

"If she was a mortal woman, she would age at a normal rate," he said. "I would not. She would grow old and die, and I would still look like I look. That would be so hard, for both of us."

About this time it occurred to me that we were still holding hands, and that his thumb was moving softly over mine in a kind of circular pattern. What are you doing? I asked myself. How awkward was this whole thing going to be?

At the same time, though, I liked it. . . .

. . . a lot.

"So you've been playing the field for three centuries," I said, trying to make something vaguely resembling a joke out of it all. "Sounds rough."

"Believe me, there have been times when I've wished it were otherwise," he said. "Times when I wished I could just give up the hunt and settle down with someone. I can't bring myself to do that, though. Not until Season is gone."

The waiter brought the pizza then, and we separated our hands. But even afterward I could feel his hand on mine as if we had never let each other go. I changed the subject, aware that I'd probably been too personal, gone too far.

And anyway, what is my deal? Here I will psychoanalyze myself in hopes of figuring out why I practically threw myself at this guy who is a) older than me and b) not quite human.

I haven't, to understate the point, had a lot of experience with boys. Or men, which Daniel clearly is.

These last few years—the dating years, according to my friends—have mostly been spent taking care of a sick, and then dying, mother. Friday night, Saturday night? Just as dateless as the rest of the week. Sure, I saw guys at school, during the day. But when school was over I had to rush home, leaving little to non-existent social time. The occasional party, the occasional groping post-adolescent. Not exactly "seventeen and never been kissed," but close enough.

That being the case, is it surprising that I seem to be hurling myself toward the first male who gives me the time of day? Hormones are hormones, after all, and mine are just as demanding as the next female's. There have, of course, been other males who have looked at me for more than twenty seconds. Mace, I think, I could have had in a heartbeat, if I'd wanted him. But, in spite of the physique, sooo not my type. And Scott has made it clear—not out loud, but through glances and signs and the occasional too-long hug—that he might toss Brandy aside for me, but I couldn't do that to her even if I wanted that. Which I so don't.

But Daniel—unattached, mature, attractive . . . I mean, what's not to like?

Did I mention mature? It keeps coming back to

that, doesn't it? And yet my inner Freud says, didn't your father die when you were very young? And didn't that make you feel abandoned as a girl, even before your mother became ill? Is it not possible that you are merely trying to fill the hole left in your heart by a father who was gone from your life all too early?

How do I answer the old Austrian? Or even Brandy, who has her own theories about things psychoanalytic but would surely be in agreement here. Yes, it's possible, Doc. Maybe even likely. But there's something to be said for the way my heart quickens when I'm around him, the way he can make me smile just by being there, the way his touch curls my toes. His scent sends those hormones racing, even when it's only a lingering aroma on the pages of his journal. This is definitely something I'd e my one-time best bud Jessica about, if I thought she'd be at all interested anymore.

But really, what could I tell her? There's this guy, and he's got magical powers, and he's three hundred years old . . . I guess this is something I just need to work out solo.

On the other hand maybe what I need is to stop thinking about this so much and just feel for a while.

Feeling would be nice. . . .

• • •

Pacific Beach was loaded with apartment complexes, large and small. In some neighborhoods almost every block had at least one, and in other parts, especially closer to the ocean, apartments greatly outnumbered single-family homes. If Season was living in this area, she had picked a high-density locale with lots of places to hide.

"She's here," Daniel said with what sounded like absolute certainty. It was midafternoon, and though they'd taken a break for lunch, he had essentially been on his feet all day, tracking, tracking.

Kerry looked at the literally dozens of dwellings she could see from this spot. "Which here?"

"I don't know," Daniel answered, and the anger was evident in his voice. "Around here the tracks go every direction. I know this is close to home for her, because she has been over just about every inch of these streets—these, and the ones nearby. Tracks are everywhere. Too many of them—I can't possibly narrow it down any further."

"So you've got, what, six square blocks? What now, door to door?"

"More like a dozen," he said. "Door to door, solo, would take weeks. And I'd be exposed the whole time."

The moment they'd shared while waiting for pizza had seemingly passed as they'd eaten and then returned to the hunt—*I'll have plenty to write in the old diary tonight, though,* Kerry thought—and they were back to business as usual. Except she couldn't quite shake the feeling that something had changed between them, possibly forever.

"Fortunately for you," she said cheerfully, "you aren't solo. Door to door probably isn't absolutely necessary, but if we've got it narrowed down to a dozen blocks, and five people she has never seen—well, four, anyway, and me, who she's only seen briefly—we can cover the neighborhood pretty well. We'll find her, Daniel. We've got her boxed in."

He thought about it for a moment. "The closer we get to her, the more I worry about you," he said. She was pretty sure that, in that instance, the "you" was specific to her and not referring to the whole group. But that might have been wishful thinking.

"It's what we're here for," she reminded

him. "I mean, there's nothing else keeping us in San Diego now, right? No jobs, no other friends. We've been stalling our families, especially Brandy, whose parents got a call about Mace and threatened to fly out here. We're in this deep, Daniel. We are here to do this thing. So let us do it."

Daniel considered a few seconds longer, but Kerry didn't see how he could possibly reach any other conclusion. "Okay," he finally said. "Let's round up the others and set a game plan."

15

The next day the stakeout was in place. *Such as it is,* Kerry thought. Three cars, six people, and one of the cars, with herself and Daniel in it, had to stay out of the immediate vicinity because they would be too easily recognized. Of course, Season usually kept to herself, Daniel reasoned, so chances were slim that she'd see them. But then, he usually worked alone too, and now he had recruited help. There was nothing to say that Season couldn't do the same, and if she had, Kerry and Daniel would be the ones they'd be watching for.

So Scott and Brandy took one car and parked it on the route that Season would most likely pass by on her way back to La Jolla, since it seemed she still frequented that community. Josh and Rebecca were roamers, cruising the

streets of the dozen blocks Daniel had identi-
fied as the ones Season used most often. Daniel
and Kerry had moved around outside the
perimeter, spending most of the day cramped
up in the car. Now that it was night, they had
parked in a busy neighborhood, near the beach
on Garnet Avenue, where restaurants, night-
clubs, and bars kept things hopping all day and
most of the night.

Everyone was connected by cell phones,
though they were instructed only to use those
in emergencies. Everyone knew that "emergency" was defined as a Season sighting.

Daniel parked in front of a store that had
already closed for the evening. Most of the
people on the sidewalks were young and fash-
ionable, drifting from one trendoid watering
hole to another. Men were dressed in jeans and
untucked shirts, high-heeled women in short
skirts with low-cut tops. The crowd was college age, or just a little older. Kerry felt a
momentary pang that she was missing out on
the fun, instead sitting here on a life-and-death
mission that she barely understood. Sure, she
was here with Daniel, not alone. But they had
been together all day, studiously ignoring the

issue of what had happened between them at lunch the day before, while those people were out laughing, eating and drinking, enjoying the San Diego summer night. She didn't have that luxury and couldn't help being a little sorry she was on this side of the windshield instead of that one. *What must a "normal" life be?* she wondered. She'd never had one, and it didn't look like she would any time soon.

"Tell me why we're here again, Daniel," she said, after the silence between them had grown uncomfortable.

"That's a complicated question," he replied with a chuckle. "Do you mean in the cosmic sense? Or the strategic one?"

"I mean, why we're doing all this. Why you don't just accept that Season is always going to be there—if not her, then someone like her—and move on with your life? Try for some happiness while you can, instead of spending all your days on the hunt?"

In the glow from neon signs and streetlights, his face, when he turned to regard her, was serious, even stern. She thought she'd pushed him too far—between the flirting at lunch the day before, and now this, she was losing her grounding, forgetting to switch on the filter that would keep her from saying and doing stupid things. "That is a tough question," he answered. "You know the facile answers. Because Season is evil. Because she destroyed my town, killed my family."

"Before you were born," Kerry reminded him.

"That's true. Have you read my journals yet?"

"Just started," Kerry said. The night was warmer than was typical for San Diego, as if the heat wave that had started up ruled the dark as well as the light, and the windows were open to let air circulate. From outside she heard a burst of laughter, causing her to look out at a group of men seemingly sharing a joke. "But I haven't had much time."

"When you make more progress you'll see that there are other reasons as well," he assured her. "As for what makes me think that I have to be the instrument of justice? That's more complicated, and I'd have to be a smarter man than I am to figure it out."

"But how do you even define justice in a case like this? Does she have to die for justice to be served? Does she have to die by your hand? Where are the boundaries?"

"My preference," Daniel said, after considering for a few moments, "would be to kill her myself. I know that's going to be difficult—if it was easy, I'd have done it long ago. But that's the ideal."

"Is there a second best?" she asked him. "Something you can settle for?"

"In fact, there is." He shifted in his seat, bumping his knees against the steering wheel. "Next year there's an event we call the Convocation, or the Witches' Convocation, more correctly. It comes around twice every millennium, or every five hundred years."

"Like a Woodstock for witches?" Kerry asked.

"More or less. Maybe more like a trade show. But with elements of Woodstock, for sure. It's a gathering. Virtually all the world's serious witches come together—a few hundred of us, all in one place. We share stories, complain about problems, offer one another help and advice. Witches go to learn new spells, to see friends and family, and so on."

Kerry did the mental math. "But you've

never been," she observed. "The last one would have been before you were born."

"That's right. I haven't. We all hear stories, though, and I've heard a lot of them. I can't wait for it."

"It does sound kind of fun," Kerry admitted. "But I don't see what it has to do with Season Howe."

"Because I haven't told you yet," Daniel teased. "One of the things that happens is that tribunals are gathered, crimes between witches dealt with. There's also a lot of politicking that goes on—this is the witch world's main chance to form alliances or partnerships, and to push various agendas."

"Now it sounds like a political convention."

Daniel nodded. Outside, a partyer with a few too many drinks under his belt bumped into the car as he made for the curb. Daniel shot him a sharp glance, then turned back to Kerry. "There is an element of that to it," he agreed. "Where Season comes into it is this: If necessary, we can convene a tribunal, effectively putting her on trial for her crimes."

"That sounds like a good thing."

"It is, to a point," Daniel said. "But there's

also the chance that she could be acquitted, just like with any trial in your world. There's also the chance that she could form a powerful enough alliance to block any tribunal. She could even use it as a platform to sway more witches over to her side—the Dark Side, to use *Star Wars* terminology. The side of chaos and destruction. If that happened, and the Convocation ended with that alliance intact, the whole world could be looking at a new Dark Age. The last Dark Age, according to all reports, was bad enough. With new technology, new weapons, and current global stresses, the world might never survive another one."

This was a lot to take in, maybe too much. "So . . . you're saying the Dark Age—as in, *the* Dark Ages, medieval times, whatever—was the result of a bunch of bad witches teaming up to make trouble?"

"That's about the size of it," Daniel said. "Look, it's getting a little raucous around here. What do you say we find another place to wait for a while?"

Kerry agreed, and he started the engine and drove around the neighborhood for a few minutes. The phone had been silent all night, and Kerry was pretty sure Season was either staying inside, or she had managed the not-so-difficult task of evading the other two searching vehicles. After circling a particular block a few times, a parking space opened up, and Daniel nosed the car into it.

"We're a block from the beach," he said. "Take a walk?"

She had hardly had a moment to go to the beach since meeting Daniel, and she realized that she missed it fiercely. "Absolutely," she said quickly. "Do we dare leave the car?"

"We'll keep the phone with us, and stay close by," Daniel promised as he opened his door. "I don't really think she's going out tonight."

"I was just thinking the same thing."

"Great minds . . ." Daniel came around to her side of the car and opened her door. Then, like a perfect gentleman, he reached for her hand and helped her out. She could have easily done it herself, but there was something unexpectedly charming about this, a hint of old-fashioned chivalry absent in the males she had known before.

"Why, thank you, sir," she said, beaming at him.

"It's my pleasure, madam," he replied.

Here on the beach, the noise on Garnet was behind them by a couple of blocks, drowned out by the gentle thunder of the surf rolling forward, collapsing on itself, and pulling back, over and over. Wind off the water carried the scents of aquatic flora and fauna and snapped away the sounds from the couple of bonfire parties spread about the beach. Water and sky were equally black, with white stars glittering overhead and glimmering in the sea of foam and moonlight.

When their feet hit the sand, they still hadn't released each other's hands. Without letting go, Kerry kicked her sandals off and picked them up with her free hand. Daniel held on, helping her maintain her balance.

But that, she knew, was only her physical balance. It was her emotional equilibrium that was dizzy now. The cool sand between her toes felt comfortable, and so did his hand in hers, and she decided that it was time for one more push. Either it would go well . . .

. . . or it wouldn't.

"So, this is all a little confusing," she said after a short while.

"What is?" Daniel asked. "The Convocation? Season?"

She gave a little laugh. "I'm past all that," she said. "No, I mean this." She gave his hand a squeeze. "Us. If there is an us. Just what exactly are we doing here?"

"Ahh," he responded. "I think I see what you're getting at. You mean what makes me think that I, an over-the-hill, overly serious geezer with a mission, would have a chance with a beautiful, lively, spirited young woman such as yourself?"

Laughing again, she kicked sand at his feet. "That wasn't exactly what I meant. But I guess it was close enough."

"Then the answer is . . . I have no idea." He stopped walking and turned to face her, releasing her hand but putting both of his own on the sides of her waist. She dropped her sandals to the ground and pressed her hands loosely against the backs of his arms, not trusting her own emotions at this moment, not confident in her own impulses. "I don't know what we're doing," he elaborated. "But I know what I want, and I hope you want the same thing. I think you do." He stopped, took a deep breath, blew it out. "I've been wrong before, though."

"I don't think you are. Not this time," Kerry assured him. "That is, if you want what I suspect you do."

He pressed his hands more firmly against her waist, then took a step forward, sliding his hands around her back and pulling her toward him. She went willingly, happily, letting him guide her to him, loving the feel of his big hands spreading across her back. At the same time, she moved her own hands up his arms and around him, across his wide shoulders, and pulled him down toward her. As if choreographed, she tilted her head back and rose up on the balls of her feet, and he leaned forward. She felt her chest press against his, broad and muscular beneath his light cotton shirt, and then his lips were on hers and his hands moved hungrily across her back. Kerry returned that hunger, and then some, and they hardly noticed as the sea surged toward them, soaking their legs, then pulled back and left them standing in the wet sand, deeper than they'd been just a moment before.

Kerry Profitt's diary, August 26

Dear Diary,
    Oh, never mind.

More later.

K.

16

My first impression of New York City, for this trip, anyway, is that they haven't finished building it yet. But it's definitely changed a lot since the last time I was here, which was, I think, 1899 or maybe spring of 1900.

I flew into LaGuardia and caught a cab into the city. I loaded my gear into the cab, and when I told the driver I was going to the Carlyle, his mouth dropped open. "I've been saving up," I told him.

"No foolin'," he said. Apparently I don't look much like your average Carlyle sort. But it's comfortable and centrally located, right next to Central Park. A good location is important when you're trying to find a single woman somewhere in America's biggest city, and you don't know where to begin.

Back to the first impression, though—it was just about dusk when I got my first good look at modern Manhattan. Tall buildings, of course, but all over the skyline are these giant cranes. It's like the Empire State Building and the Chrysler Building and those others I don't know the names of aren't enough—every building in the city has to be a skyscraper.

After the cranes, what I notice next are the lights. Millions of them, twinkling everywhere I look. Lighted windows, lighted signs, lighted billboards. The cabbie drives me through Times Square, at my request, and it's just a crazy riot of light and color. There are signs and posters plastered everywhere for Look Homeward, Angel at the Ethel Barrymore Theatre, which I guess opens this week. Tony Perkins is in it, and it seems to be the talk of the town at the moment. That and, of course, Thanksgiving, which means turkey dinners and the Macy's parade and Christmas lights, adding to the sparkle in the streets. There are people everywhere—on *the sidewalks and spilling onto the streets, dressed to the nines, laughing and having a grand time, it seems. It would be nice to join them, I think, but business before pleasure.*

After giving me the nickel tour and running up the fare at the same time, of course, the cabbie drives me to the Carlyle, which surprises me by being every bit as fancy as he had warned me. Thirty-five stories tall, all beautiful art-deco design, a big fire roaring in the fireplace and formal-dressed staff all over the place—pretty tony for an old witch. But I can afford it, so why not?

In fact, I'm sitting in one of its deluxe beds right now and ready to try it out for real. So I'll set this aside for the night and get back to it when there's something new to report.

I remain,

Daniel Blessing, November 26, 1957

Kerry put the leather book down and jabbed the power button on her laptop, hoping its hum wouldn't disturb Rebecca. She and

Daniel had stayed on the beach, exploring each other with lips and tongues and hands and eyes, until midnight, when Scott had called Daniel's cell. They had all headed home then, recognizing a major flaw in their plan—that Season could easily slip through their already loose net while they slept—but also accepting the obvious truth that people parked overnight in a residential neighborhood might attract the unwanted attention of the police.

Who still, presumably, wanted to talk to them about Mace's murder.

Kerry Profitt's diary, August . . . oh, who cares.

I'm writing this in bed, with the machine on my lap—hence the name "laptop," duh—while he is in bed in the next room, probably trying to ignore Josh's snores.

I'm only guessing that Josh snores, but it seems like he would.

But the important fact of my life is not Josh snoring. Rather, it is that he—should that be HƎ?—is sleeping just twenty feet from where I am sleeping. Or, not sleeping. In my case.

If I were a different person I'd be scribbling the

name "Daniel" across the inside cover of my note-book now, a hundred times, in different colored pens. Some with hearts around them, or flowers.

I'm not that girl, though. I'm laptop chick, ever so much more sophisticated.

Besides, I can just cut-and-paste.

Daniel

Daniel

Daniel

Daniel

See? Maybe loses some of the visceral impact. But I'm still all squooshy with visceral, anyway, from earlier, on the beach. I think my toes are perma-nently pruned, and did I mention that Pacific Ocean water is cold? I mean, at the moment I was sort of disregarding the part of my body called feet in favor of other parts. But when we stopped, I realized that I was, like, frostbitten or something.

Okay, not. But damn cold just the same. Teeth chattering, even.

Which is when Daniel did the coolest thing. Or one of them, anyway.

He got down on one knee, giving me momentary proposal jitters, I must say, and then he took my feet—crusty and sandy from beach and saltwater, and yuck!—in his hands, one at a time, and held them. But the thing is, when he held them, his hands generated some kind of warming field, like they were mini-toasters and my cold, aching feet were the bread. After a few seconds in his hands, the cold and the pain went away, and my feet felt completely rejuvenated.

He's a one-man spa, that Daniel Blessing.

So we got home and talked for a while about the fruitlessness of the day's long, long stakeout. But we don't have enough people to pull different shifts, so we pretty much have to be out there as many hours as we can, and just tough it out. Meanwhile, Daniel and I were trying hard not to make googly eyes at each other, and we managed not to tell the others what had happened, even though I want to, but on the way home we agreed that it might make them feel awkward, and maybe we should hold off telling anyone for a while.

So then we went to bed. We were able to clasp hands, just for a moment, as we passed in the hall. That was it.

Fortunately I can still feel his lips on mine, still taste him, still remember the crush of his hands on me.

Giddy? Me?

Forcing myself not to write in here until after R

had gone to sleep because I was afraid I might just start giggling, or crying, or both, and she'd want to know what was going on and I'd have to tell her. So I got out the journals and skipped around for a bit, finally finding what looked like another story instead of just the "woke up, didn't find her, went to bed" reportage of so many days, read that for a while. Until R's breathing was regular. I'm sure she's out now.

So here I am. Instead of being crushing school-girl with my friends, I'm being crushing schoolgirl with a box full of wires and . . . well, whatever is inside computers. Chips? Whatever they look like.

It's all magic to me. I touch keys and words appear on the screen. Magic. Daniel touches my feet, and they warm and stop hurting. Magic. Daniel's mouth presses against mine and every worry I ever had flies out of my head. Magic.

Daniel? You're not just playing a game, are you?
silence
silence
silence
Didn't think so.

More later.

K.

New York is a funny town.

So many people. I'm certain that Season is here somewhere, but I roamed the city all day and didn't pick up a trace of her. Just about wore through my shoes, though—I'll likely need a new pair before I leave.

The good thing about New York is that you can buy anything here. No problem finding a new pair of shoes. The only hard part might be deciding: loafers, wing tips, what? I guess it'll depend on my mood when I'm in the store.

After having spent all day wandering around in the cold, though—and I'm talking COLD—I decided to check out the balloon preparation for the big parade tomorrow. I braved wind and weather (and skies that promise rain, I fear, for tomorrow) to hike the Upper West Side, watching colorful stretches of rubber slowly take shape. Mighty Mouse, clowns, Popeye the Sailor, a tremendous dachshund, toy soldiers, and other fanciful forms began to billow and shake as gigantic helium tanks filled them. The streets were crowded with revelers and volunteers, the latter working to control their balloons, the former hindering that effort, as often as not.

One old geezer buttonholed me as I watched, anxious for any target for his stories. "I was at the end of the route in '30," he told me. "Right in front of Macy's. In those days, they let the balloons go at parade's end, you know. Just let 'em float away. Most of 'em popped before they cleared the store—noise was terrible, and the bits of rubber raining down stank something awful too. But some of them got away, and Macy's had a reward out for their safe return—one year, two tugboats each caught an end of one of them wiener dogs, and pulled it in two."

"That's fascinating," I told the codger. But I tried to work my way clear of him because I was getting a strange feeling. One I didn't like a bit. Was it Season? I thought it over for a couple of moments, but no, it wasn't that. I was still trying to figure it when I heard a woman scream, not too far away—around the corner, I thought, and about half a block down.

A couple of us took off running toward the sound, but I was the fastest. When I reached her—forty, perhaps, nicely dressed, in a fur-lined coat, with boots and gloves to protect against the chill—she shouted something about her purse and a guy with a knife. She pointed down the block, and I just kept running.

I don't know what happened behind me, if the other men who ran toward her stopped to comfort her, or to call the cops, or what. All I knew is that a few minutes later I was on a block that seemed hundreds of miles removed from the swank Upper West Side blocks where the parade balloons were. Here the brownstones were run down, with broken windows covered by boards, and trash in the streets. There seemed to be no one out. I could see the blue glow of television sets in a couple of windows, and hear radios blaring from others, but there wasn't a soul to be seen.

Part of me wanted to give up, to turn around. The lady had a fur, she could probably afford the loss of the purse and whatever dough was inside it. And if the guy who hiked her purse lived in this neighborhood, chances were that he'd just gotten away with more than he usually saw in a month. But there was a matter of principle, too. A thief is a thief, whether he steals from rich or poor.

I had touched the lady as I ran past her, though, so it wasn't a terribly difficult thing to track the progress of her purse. Eventually that trail led me to an alley, and in the alley were a half dozen hoodlums, counting out their take. Leonard Bernstein's West Side Story opened on Broadway this year, and these guys could have been extras from the rumble scene, Sharks or Jets in their leather jackets and pomaded hair.

And, I was to learn momentarily, switchblades.

One of them looked up and saw me. "You lost or something, Pops?" he asked.

"Pops," I said. "That's funnier than you know."

"I didn't mean it funny," he said back. "You guys think it sounded funny?"

They all agreed that I was the only

one who found it funny in the least. Which only made sense, considering I was the only one who knew that I was old enough to be this punk's great-great-grandfather, at the very least.

"Anyhoo," the spokesman said after they had discussed it for a while, "this here is our alley, and unless you have some business with us, I think you oughta scram."

"I do have business with you," I said. "That purse you've got. I've come to take it back to its owner."

They looked at one another then, as if surprised by what I said. I guess they were. They couldn't have known I'd be able to track it this far. They thought they were home safe.

I guess they still did think that. "He's a funny man," the spokesman said. "A truly funny man, is old Pops."

"I'm not being funny," I said. "I'd like the purse, please. And all the money that was in it."

This is when the switchblades came out. Snap, crackle, pop, like the cereal, and *suddenly all eight guys had steel in their hands.*

I just looked at them, still hoping they'd do it the easy way. "The purse, please," I repeated.

The spokesman grabbed the purse from the one holding it, and waved it toward me. "Whynchoo come get it?" he asked. I'm just putting it down the way it sounded. Whynchoo.

"If that's the way you want it," I said. "I was hoping to spare you some trouble."

They looked at one another again. This time a couple of them looked nervous. I think they were getting the idea that I wasn't someone who was going to back down easily. Since they were used to people who did back down easily, that meant I had some kind of gimmick. Maybe a gun, maybe some friends, they didn't know what. But some secret weapon, because no one would be foolish enough to face down eight switchblade hoods without one.

In fact I did have one. Not any of the

ones they might have thought. But a good one, just the same.

There were any number of ways it could have gone. I wanted them to remember it, though. I wanted them to learn something from it. I didn't want them to write it off later as some kind of hallucination, bad liquor or dope, or whatever else they might have imbibed that night. I wanted it to seem as natural as possible. So instead of just knocking them all out, or lifting them off their feet and slamming them magically into the walls of the alley, I decided to go hand-to-hand.

Of course, my hand was a little stronger than their hand. Even with the knives, which would never touch me. But they didn't have to know that. All they'd know was that a seemingly unarmed civilian could stand up to the bunch of them, and win.

I advanced on them at a regular walking pace. Some of the switchblade-wielding fists shook now, as they realized that this was turning ugly. Maybe they were afraid they'd have to kill me, and while they were hoodlums and punks, I thought they probably weren't killers by nature. Maybe they were just plain afraid.

I started with the spokesman, because he annoyed me the most. Easily dodging his knife, I caught his jaw with a right hook, followed with a jab to the gut and then an uppercut to the chin. He went down hard. Now the others were all stabbing at me, but I took them one by one, letting their blades slip past me. A few punches here, a couple of karate chops there, some judo throws for variety. Finally the last two broke out running, down the alley away from me. But that was okay. I wasn't going to chase. I gathered up all the money the ones left behind had on them, on the theory that even if it hadn't come from the purse, they'd stolen it from someone, and tucked it inside the lady's wallet. Then I left them in the alley. They'd wake up in a few hours, never again quite so confident, I hoped, in their own invulnerability.

I found the lady about where I'd left her, answering questions from a uniformed cop who wrote slowly, and with obvious difficulty, in a little notebook. Gave her the purse. Explained that it had been dropped, several blocks away, and I hoped she wasn't too inconvenienced. Ignored the look the cop shot me, like if I wasn't the snatcher, I was probably in league with him. Back on 90th I caught a cab back to the Carlyle, and here I am. It's starting to rain outside.

Interesting day. Interesting city. No Season.

I remain,

Daniel Blessing, November 27, 1957

17

"You get any sleep?"

Scott looked at Kerry like she was some kind of lab specimen. Then again, she felt like some kind of lab specimen, so maybe that was how she did look. When she'd been in the bathroom, she hadn't quite been able to focus on the mirror, which, judging from Scott's greeting, was probably a bonus.

"Not much," she admitted. "I was reading."

"You were?" Rebecca asked. "I didn't even know."

Because you could sleep through nuclear war, Kerry thought. *Or a Soundgarden concert, at least.* She just shrugged and tried to smile, though.

She felt strange this morning. As if she was the same person she had been yesterday, but everything around her had changed. Like she had gone to bed at home, but had woken up in a foreign country. She didn't know the language, the customs, the lay of the land. But she'd made the trip willingly—buying her own ticket, bringing her passport. A strange feeling, that was the only way to describe it.

"Must have been a good book," Scott said. "Keeping you awake and all."

"One of Daniel's journals. It's pretty interesting reading."

"Does it have any advice in it about how to survive a stakeout?" Brandy asked, coming into the kitchen from the bedroom she shared with Scott. "Because all day in a car . . . I thought my legs were permanently frozen in a sitting position."

"You took enough bathroom breaks," Scott teased. "You could have walked around a little more then."

"I'll have to today," Brandy shot back. "I go back into that mini-mart, they're going to start charging me rent."

"Josh suggested using a bottle or a can," Rebecca offered. "I told him if I even saw him bring a bottle or can into the car, I was throwing him out."

Brandy cracked up. "Good for you."

"That's how they do it in real life, I guess," Scott said. "Not that this isn't, you know, . . ."

Rebecca flapped her hands at him. "I think that's how it's done in those crime books and movies Josh likes," she replied. "I don't know about real life. I just know I'm not sitting there while Josh whips out a soda bottle."

Daniel wandered in then, hair still mussed from sleeping and a crease from his pillow on his face. Kerry liked it. As she learned more about him, sometimes it was hard to remember that he was human—not quite like her, obviously, but still, at his core. A pillow mark on his face, though—that was as human as it got. He was a long-lived, incredibly powerful man, but he was still a man.

She'd have to remember to kiss that cheek later, where she saw the crease. Maybe some other spots, too.

"I don't blame you a bit, Rebecca," he said as he rummaged in the cabinet for a clean cup. "This is serious business, I'm afraid. But just as I don't want any of you to try to engage Season on your own, I don't want you to injure yourselves, or to be any more put out than is absolutely necessary. We'll stake her out, but we won't kill ourselves doing it, okay?"

"We're already about as put out as we can be," Brandy observed. "Unless you don't count our lives being turned upside down and put in danger."

"Oh, I do," Daniel said. He poured coffee from the pot into his cup, took a sip, grimaced. Kerry had noticed that he nearly always tasted it, even though he invariably put in sugar afterward. *Old habits,* she figured. "Believe me, I know how seriously I've inconvenienced all of you."

"But if we get Season," Kerry put in, "then it's all worth it. Everything. Even . . . even Mace."

She felt Brandy's gaze burning into her. "You sure you want to go there?"

"I feel terrible about Mace, Brandy, you know I do. But Season is responsible for so many deaths, so much sorrow and loss. If we could stop her, think of everyone we'd be helping. All of her future victims."

"We're on board," Scott assured her. "Doesn't mean we have to be thrilled about it. But you don't see any of us turning away, do you?"

"Josh tries to bring a bottle into my car," Rebecca said, trying to sound hard-boiled, "I'll turn him away."

"Yeah, you talk like a tough cookie!" Josh called from behind the closed bathroom door. "We'll just see how tough you really are when the chips are down."

Rebecca laughed and blushed, lifting her breakfast dishes from the table and carrying them to the sink. So far, Kerry decided, she was impressed with all of her friends, for even sticking it out this long, and for being willing to go to all this trouble.

The chips, she was pretty sure, had been down for a long time.

The shopping center was wood-sided, painted brown, reasonably busy. It wasn't much more than a glorified strip mall containing a coffee shop and a bagel shop, a drugstore, office and pet supplies stores, a couple of restaurants, and at one end, a supermarket. But there was enough traffic in and out so no one really noticed that one nondescript Ford Taurus had parked in the slender shade offered by a tree and hadn't moved for a long time.

Anyone looking into the car, though, might notice that the couple in the front seat was locked in passionate embrace, as often as not.

"Should we really be doing this?" Kerry asked when they broke once. It was midafternoon; they'd been on the stakeout since eight that morning. The windows were half open so the occasional breeze could help cool the car's interior. They'd taken one break for ice-cream cones, and a couple of others to replenish their supply of cold bottled water. "The others . . ."

"We don't kiss so loudly that we wouldn't hear the phone," Daniel assured her. "But if you want to stop . . ."

"That's not what I said." At the moment, she could hardly imagine a more pleasant way to pass the time than sitting and talking with Daniel Blessing, interrupted from time to time by a bout of feverish kissing.

"Tonight," Daniel announced, somewhat abruptly, "we'll tell them."

For a moment Kerry was confused. "Tell them . . . oh. *Tell* them. About us."

"There's no reason we should have to keep

it a secret," Daniel said. "We're both adults. You're young, yes, but you're as mature a woman as I've ever known."

Kerry felt herself crimsoning. "Thanks. I guess . . . I guess I had to grow up fast, with my mom and dad in the conditions they were in."

"You've done an admirable job." He traced a pattern on her knee with his finger. She wore khaki shorts and a red cotton T-shirt, almost the color she figured her face had turned, because in spite of the August heat, they couldn't run the air-conditioning the whole time they were parked, and his touch was cool, comforting. Somehow Daniel stayed crisp in a white linen shirt with the long sleeves rolled up and faded jeans. "I told you before, I've been with a few women over the years."

She didn't necessarily like to think about that. "Yeah."

"But none of them . . . ever . . . have meant what you have come to mean to me, Kerry. You . . ."

He paused, and she waited for him to finish his sentence. He worked his jaw, she could see the little worm of a scar under it twitch, but nothing came out.

Finally she decided to take him off the hook, finally allowing herself to say what she'd been holding inside, not even certain of her own feelings until just this moment. "I can't say I've been with a lot of guys," she said. "And obviously never with an age difference like we have. But I think I feel the same way. Like there's something about you that I just respond to, that I'm at ease with. It's hard to remember when you weren't in my life, and hard to imagine a future without you in it." She laughed, suddenly even more nervous than she'd expected. Whenever she'd had this kind of conversation in her head, growing up, it had all flowed so easily. "God, isn't this the kind of talk we should be having six months from now, maybe? I'm so bad at this I don't even know what the timing is supposed to be like."

"It's supposed to be whatever feels right," Daniel said, squeezing her leg. "And this does."

"So tonight?" Kerry asked, aware that maybe she was, once again, about to push too hard. "When we tell them? Do you think maybe we can get Rebecca and Josh to share a room?"

Daniel smiled at her, obviously pleased by the suggestion. "It's worth a try," he said.

He leaned toward her, drawing her closer with subtle pressure on her leg, and their lips were almost in contact when his phone chirped at them. He raised an eyebrow in annoyance. "Great timing."

"It's not like we haven't had a chance to kiss today," Kerry reminded him, biting back her own disappointment. "Or like we won't have plenty of time later."

Fishing the phone from his pocket, Daniel pouted. "But I wanted one now."

Kerry stretched toward him and planted one on his cheek, right where the pillow-crease had been. "There you go," she said. "Now answer your phone."

"Pick up, pick up, pick up," Rebecca pleaded, listening to Daniel's phone ring.

"Trying to drive here," Josh said with a growl. He had the wheel of the Civic, and he wore an unpleasant scowl as he tried to maneuver around a Buick that had lurched from an apartment complex's lot into their way. "You want to put the kibosh on the whining?"

Pick up, pick up, pick up, Rebecca thought anxiously. Josh's mood was foul enough that she didn't want to aggravate it any more. But—

"Hello," Daniel's voice spoke in her ear.

"We found her!" Rebecca realized she'd shouted it, but didn't care. She could almost feel Josh's glare.

"Where are you?"

She glanced at their surroundings. "Heading toward the water, so west, I guess, on Emerald."

"She's driving?" Daniel asked.

"Yes. Driving."

"In what?"

"A car." Rebecca said, flustered. She'd known a minute ago, but the tension and excitement of the chase were getting to her.

"Forest green Nissan Maxima," Josh informed her.

She relayed the message, and added, "We were driving down Emerald, and she passed us, going the other way. Josh pulled over, then turned around. She's a couple of blocks ahead of us."

"Okay, good job, Rebecca," Daniel said sharply. "I'm going to alert Brandy and Scott now. I'll check back in a minute."

He broke the connection, and Rebecca put the phone in her lap. Two- and three-story apartment buildings flashed past her window; the fronds of tall palms strobed the sunlight that raked across the windshield. Ahead she could see a van and a big black SUV. "Where is she?" she asked Josh. "I don't see her."

"Don't sweat it, I have her," Josh assured her. "I'm hanging back so she doesn't make us." He tossed her a sideways grin. "You act like I don't know what I'm doing."

"You watch a lot of movies, read some books," Rebecca countered. She was fully aware that her anxiety was making her edgier than usual, more argumentative. But she had every right to be edgy. They were chasing a killer—and worse, a killer with unknown magical powers. "I'm not sure that makes you a genuine expert on surveillance techniques."

Josh's grin turned into an unpleasant sneer. She had always liked Josh, even when the rest of their housemates found him a bit obnoxious. But now that he was in his element—or what he believed was his element, even though he had no particular experience with, or real-life knowledge of, the seamier side of life—he got all bent out of shape when she dared to question his abilities. As if to prove her wrong, he mashed down hard on the accelerator and the car lunged ahead. At the same time he twisted the wheel to the left, swerving into the oncoming traffic lane, which was blessedly empty. He stayed on the gas, pulling ahead of the van, then cutting back into the correct lane. The van's horn bleated, the SUV in the other lane ticked to the side as if worried about being hit. But three blocks ahead of them, just making a right turn, she spotted the green Nissan.

Josh glanced at her, wordlessly triumphant.

18

Brandy flipped the phone open as soon as it rang. "Hey," she said.

"She's on the move." Daniel's voice, brittle with anxiety. "On Emerald, headed west. Toward you."

"Okay," Brandy answered, not sure what other response was needed. If any. She and Scott were parked on Mission, near Beryl, on the route one would take from Pacific Beach to La Jolla.

"Dark green Nissan Maxima," Daniel added.

"We'll watch for her," Brandy promised.

"Don't get right behind her," Daniel warned. "Let her get a few car lengths ahead. Josh and Rebecca will be following too, so you should both take turns pulling up and slipping back. Make sure she doesn't see the same car in her rearview the whole time."

"I got it," Brandy said.

"We're on the way over. I'll check back in a few." Daniel signed off, and she folded the phone. Scott looked at her, curiosity on his face.

"What's up?"

"Get ready for action, Scott. She's coming this way." Brandy repeated the details Daniel had given her. "Let's not lose her this time," she said. "I'd sure love to get all this over with."

Scott nodded as he turned the key in the ignition and gunned the engine. The air inside the car was charged now; the urgency of imminent contact, the anticipation of some kind of conclusion to the summer's madness striking them both. "That makes two of us."

A couple of minutes later the phone rang again. "It's Rebecca," their housemate's voice said when Brandy answered. "She's not coming your way after all. She turned south on Mission, not north."

"We're on it," Brandy acknowledged. She hung up and filled Scott in.

So Season wasn't heading for La Jolla this

time—or to the freeway, at least, not right away. South on Mission would take her through Pacific Beach, and into Mission Beach. But that would become a dead end; eventually she'd have to turn inland, crossing Mission Bay. Then she could go out Point Loma, which would trap her on a long peninsula, or toward downtown and the freeways.

Scott pulled out of the parking place, waited for a break in traffic, and performed an illegal U-turn in the middle of the block. Now he was headed south on Mission, as well. He stomped on the gas and the car shot forward. Traffic was light, but there were cars on the road, and he wove between lanes to get around them. Brandy found herself clutching her seat, trying not to show fear. They'd have to live through the chase if they would ever get a chance to die at Season's hands, she knew.

Of course, there was the other option, too—the one where they defeated Season and ended the summer in triumph. She hadn't been willing to give much consideration to that scenario, unwilling to get her hopes up. Life, she had found, was somewhat less disappointing if she didn't expect too much out of it to begin with. Allowing herself to imagine that she'd be some kind of hero, would help save the world—*okay, not the world,* she thought, *but at least lives, someone's world*—had been too ambitious for her to even consider.

Now, though, she couldn't help it. She had the sense that some kind of conclusion was coming, some ultimate confrontation. Either they'd walk away from it or Season would, but no way would the status quo be unchanged at the end.

So she hung on and let Scott drive, silently watching the road ahead, his hands tight on the wheel. A trickle of sweat ran down the side of his face, dripping from beneath the temple-piece of his glasses. Brandy worried a little about him, about how he'd deal with this whole thing. He was a smart guy, and she loved him, really loved him like no other boyfriend she'd had. But confrontation wasn't his forte. He was smart but not strong, not in the physical sense, although he was no weakling, either—no Mace, but no Josh, either, and soccer had given him great legs—but in the emotional sense. When life battered him around, he didn't bounce back easily. Even something as seemingly minor as a disagreement in traffic—someone cutting him off or flipping him off—unsettled him for at least a day.

She'd been pleasantly surprised, so far, about how well he'd handled all this, with Daniel and Mace and everything. When things turned really bad, he seemed able to rise to meet the challenges. But she couldn't help wondering when he'd reach his breaking point, when it would all just be too much for him. Judging from the expression on his face now—lips clamped together, eyes wide, jaw as tight as a violin string—that time just might be close. She'd have to keep an eye on him.

"There's Josh and Beck," he said a few minutes later. Brandy saw them too, in the rented Civic they drove.

"We should pass them," she said. "So when she looks in her mirror—"

"I know," Scott interrupted. Brandy had already explained the theory, when reporting what Daniel had told her. She guessed the stress was getting to her too.

"I know, sorry."

"Yeah," he said. "Anyway, that's what I'm doing." He pulled even with the other car, and

Brandy waved at Josh and Rebecca. Josh made an ushering gesture with his hand, indicating that they should pull ahead. He had an unlit cigarette clamped between his teeth. Rebecca wouldn't let him smoke while she was in the car, but it looked like he'd been chewing on it. Brandy thought she could see flecks of tobacco on his chin.

Brandy and Scott pulled ahead, though, and all her attention was on the dark green sedan a block or so ahead of them, with only a driver inside.

"That's got to be her," Scott said.

"Yeah," Brandy agreed softly, more nervous than ever now that Season was in view again. This time there would be no losing her, she determined. This time it would all play out to the end. One way or another.

Suddenly every vehicle in San Diego was in Pacific Beach, either stuck in traffic on Garnet or trying to cross it. That was how it seemed to Kerry, anyway. She drove Daniel's car. He had his hands full with his cell, trying to coordinate the movements of three different vehicles, all in pursuit of a fourth, and he'd spread a city map on his lap. He tried to anticipate where Season might be headed, based on where she was. Kerry knew that was a fool's game—Season had proven her unpredictability plenty of times in the past, and could as easily turn around and head right back where she'd come from as continue on any given path. But she didn't bother to share her opinion with Daniel, who, after all, knew his enemy far better than she did.

Ahead, the traffic light turned green, and she started inching forward even before the car in front of her had moved. But three cars in front of that, a pick-up truck with surfboards spiking from the bed was trying to turn left, and sat at the light waiting for a break in the oncoming traffic. By the time the truck had passed through the light, it was turning yellow again, then red. She had moved up all of one space.

"She's not doing this, is she?" Kerry asked, only half-joking.

"What, manipulating the traffic? No, I think that's beyond even her abilities," Daniel replied. "That's the problem with traffic, it can't be controlled. Too much human element. It's barely contained chaos. Almost makes one long for the days of traffic cops, standing in the streets directing the flow."

"Or horses and buggies?" Kerry teased.

"Say what you will," Daniel said. "There were definite advantages. Quieter, safer, less polluting. The world has given up a lot in the name of progress."

"But we don't have to worry about stepping in horse manure when we cross the street," Kerry pointed out.

"That's true. Then, though, you didn't have to worry about global climate change or growing holes in the ozone layer. You didn't have to worry that you were breathing in carcinogens every day. And that's without even bringing nuclear arms or biological weapons into the equation. Life is easier now, in many ways, and safer in some. But in others, the world has gone completely, screamingly insane."

The light changed again, and Daniel fell silent as Kerry silently urged the cars in front of her to just go straight already. And it worked. This time, she made it through the light. Ahead, Garnet had the undisputed right of way for several blocks, so it was relatively clear sailing.

"Do you really think that?" she asked after awhile. "That the world is insane?"

Daniel considered the question for a long moment. "In some ways, I said. And the answer is, yes, I do. Certainly, there have been remarkable improvements, amazing technological advances. We've essentially beaten the worst diseases of history—plague, polio, whooping cough, and so on. We can vaccinate against measles and chicken pox. These things used to cripple and kill, and now they're merely inconvenient, if that. But we've also changed the world in ways we don't even understand, so that we have to deal with new cancers, with Ebola, with AIDS, with SARS. We've poisoned the air and water. We build nuclear power plants that have the potential to kill tens of thousands if something goes wrong. In many ways, large and small, from the individual to the corporation to government, we keep inventing new ways to kill, new ways to tyrannize, new ways to destroy people's lives." He chuckled dryly. "I'm sorry, Kerry, I don't mean to pontificate."

"That's okay," she said. Listening to him talk helped her cope with the frustrations of the traffic.

"No, it's not. We have other things on our plate right now." He punched some buttons on the cell phone, listened for a second. Then, "Brandy, where are you? Good, good. We'll be there in a few minutes; just trying to get through traffic."

After he hung up, he pointed at a stop light ahead, at Mission Boulevard. "Left on Mission," he told her.

"Okay," she said. She really did find his diatribe intriguing. When most people talked about the differences between older days and the present, she knew, they were only basing their opinions on what they'd read or heard. He had actually lived through the whole thing, though—the settling of America, the westward expansion, the rise and fall of global powers. He was history made flesh.

But thinking about his flesh made her mind veer in other directions, and she shook her head, not wanting to let herself get distracted with thoughts of that. Plenty of time later. Right now she had to drive a car. Daniel was on the phone again, with Rebecca this time, when Kerry made the left onto Mission.

Daniel continued to direct her, and she went where he told her to—left, left, right. Through Crown Point and across the bay on a narrow bridge, then they were on wide avenues and moving fast. Past Sea World, and eventually onto I-5, heading south, but then an abrupt turn onto I-8, going east. That way was the desert and the rest of the country, eventually. Kerry found herself wondering how far they'd go today. Was the witch finally leaving San Diego behind? Part of her gloried at that idea—it would be over then, for her.

But Daniel would go too, wouldn't he? Continuing the hunt.

At Daniel's urging, she sped up, and soon she had the other two cars in sight. They slowed a little, letting her pass, acknowledging her and Daniel as they did so.

And then she could see Season, up ahead, cruising along in her dark green car. Daniel put a hand on Kerry's leg and squeezed. "No closer," he said quietly. That made sense—if she could see Season, then Season could see them. She hung back.

In the city of El Cajon, a few miles east of San Diego, the green car exited the freeway. Josh was back in front by this time. He flipped on his turn signal and followed her, and the other two cars did the same. "It's good we have three cars to work her," Daniel said. "She obviously left Pacific Beach the hard way to try to spot, or avoid, pursuit. I don't think she's seen us yet, but she still might. We'll need to be very careful on these roads."

El Cajon was a small city, and traffic there was nowhere near as heavy as it had been back in San Diego. All three vehicles stayed well behind Season's. Daniel was silent now, grimly focused on the Nissan ahead of them. The three chase cars did a dance, each taking the lead for a while, then falling back to let a different one move closer—never sticking to a pattern, but changing things up each time. Now and again one would pull into a parking lot, and then out again, or stop by the side of the road, only to pull back out after the other two had passed. The last thing anyone wanted was for Season to get stuck at a light long enough for them to catch up to her, to risk stopping right next to her or being obvious about holding back.

The streets Season chose became increasingly empty. She led them away from El Cajon's small downtown area, through residential neighborhoods where the streets were lined with small cottages or faded apartment complexes in shades of salmon or aquamarine. Overgrown yards, sometimes with cars parked in them, were not uncommon here. Fences tended to be chain-link, in various states of repair. Behind some of them, dogs stood guard or lazed in the sun. Being inland and therefore farther from the coast, El Cajon was even more brutally hot than San Diego, and there weren't many people on the streets, but Kerry spotted a few, sitting on shaded porches or walking on the sidewalks under sun hats or, in one instance, an umbrella.

"You have any idea where she's going?" she asked Daniel.

She could see his shrug from the corner of her eye. "No clue," he said. "Up to no good, I'm sure."

"Doesn't that go without saying?"

The question was answered in another couple of minutes, though. Daniel's cell rang, and when he answered, Kerry could make out

Brandy's voice, which sounded agitated. Daniel listened for a moment, thanked her, and disconnected. "She's stopping," he told Kerry. "Brandy and Scott are driving past, Rebecca and Josh are stopping behind her."

"What do we do?"

The other cars had already turned a corner that Kerry had not yet reached. Daniel pointed to the parking lot of a strip mall, before the corner, on the left-hand side of the street. "Pull in there," he said. "We'll get closer on foot."

She did as she was directed, parking in front of a taco stand, and they both got out. Daniel kept his phone in his hand. He punched a button. "Rebecca," he said. "Where is she?"

He frowned as he listened to her response, then he put away the phone and looked at Kerry. "There's an herbalist around the corner," he explained. "She's gone in there. Picking up supplies for some kind of spell, most likely."

Anxiety gnawed at Kerry's stomach, as if she'd swallowed a mouse. They were close now, as close as they'd been since that night in the kitchen when Daniel was too weak to give his all. A battle might be only moments away. She wanted it, ached for an end to Daniel's long quest. But was he strong enough now? And if he wasn't, what then? She hardly dared to imagine. "What now? Do we just go in there after her?"

"Three reasons why we don't do that," Daniel said. "One, we don't know who's in there. An herbalist may well be a cover for a witch, maybe an ally of hers. Two, we don't know if she spotted us and is trying to lead us into a trap. She may be watching the street right now from inside, waiting for us to make our move. Three, we don't know the territory. We've had no time to plan, to scout out escape routes, to know what cover there might be. Going in there now could be suicide."

Kerry was confused. "Then why have we followed her all this way?"

"Because we found her," he said simply. "We're not losing her again. That just isn't happening."

19

But they did.

Season stayed in the shop less than five minutes. Kerry and Daniel made their way around the corner and had taken up positions in the recessed doorway of an empty, boarded-up storefront. They could see the Civic up ahead, and Season's Nissan, parked right in front of a shop with a green painted sign that read HERBS 'R' US: REMEDIES AND ROMANCE, and farther ahead, Scott's RAV4. But Season's abrupt reappearance took them by surprise. Daniel and Kerry both had to turn away from the shop, facing into the doorway of the vacant store. They stayed there until they heard engines starting, and then the squeal of tires as Season pulled hurriedly away from the curb.

As soon as she was gone, Daniel grabbed

Kerry's hand. "Come on!" he urged. His phone rang, and he answered it as they ran for the car. "I know!" he shouted. "Stay on her!"

By the time they were back in Daniel's Taurus, though, Kerry once again driving, Brandy had called to tell them that Season was gone.

She had made a quick right at the first corner, then a sudden left into an alley. Scott hadn't wanted to be so obvious as to follow her down the alley while she was still in it, so Brandy called Rebecca, intending for that car to go straight instead of making the right. She and Scott would go past the alley and then left, and whichever way Season turned when she reached the alley's end, one of the cars would be near by.

Except what Season did, apparently, was to go partway down the alley, then back out and go back down the original street, in the opposite direction. Both cars were more than a block away by this time, and Kerry and Daniel, who had started at a disadvantage, weren't close enough yet to catch her.

"Do you think she saw us?" Kerry asked after Daniel explained what had happened.

"Maybe," he said. "Or maybe she's just being careful. She would know that if anyone had been following, her few minutes in the store would have given them time to catch up, maybe even lay a trap."

"I guess it wasn't her trap, though," Kerry observed.

"I called it wrong," he admitted. "Couldn't be sure, though."

"Better safe?"

"Exactly."

"So what now?" she wondered.

"Back to I-8," he said. "As fast as you can. Let's assume she's heading back home, and not away from the city." He began punching buttons on the phone. "I'll tell the others."

Ten minutes later, they had her again. She had taken a roundabout way back to the freeway, apparently hoping to shake anyone tailing her. Rebecca and Josh were the farthest back, and when they saw her coming up fast behind them they called the others. Daniel and Kerry pulled off the freeway all together, so she wouldn't recognize them when she passed. The other two cars stayed on her, and Kerry just re-entered at the same place, so within a very few minutes they were all behind her again. Kerry felt a powerful sense of relief, as if it was all over.

Which, of course, it isn't, she thought. *It hasn't even really begun.*

Forty minutes later, having gone back into Pacific Beach through La Jolla—prompting Daniel to point out that she hadn't taken a direct route anywhere—Season was back on Emerald, with Josh and Rebecca not far behind. She made a right on Everts, and pulled into the driveway of a small clapboard bungalow, at the corner of the alley that ran up the block between Emerald and Felspar—Pacific Beach's east-west streets being named after minerals. This time, Rebecca and Josh drove past, and the other two cars stopped a block away.

"Isn't that more or less where you picked her up in the first place?" Daniel asked when they called in the report. He listened, nodding, then said, "Okay, sit tight. We're on the way." He made another quick call, telling Brandy and Scott to stay where they were, motor running, just in case. Then he turned to Kerry.

"Okay, drive past the house. Not too fast,

not too slow. Just like you're out for a drive with no special destination in mind."

"But won't she see us?" Kerry wondered.

"She might," Daniel said. "If she's looking. Chance we have to take. I need to check out her place."

He sounded a bit too casual about it for her tastes, but Kerry did as she was told. She pulled away from the curb and drove at a slow, steady speed past the bungalow. Its exterior walls were painted white, with brown trim. A front porch seemed to sag under the weight of an old overstuffed chair that had suffered the elements for too long. A screen door was closed, but the heavier door behind that stood open. It looked like the kind of place a college student might live in, Kerry thought, or a young professional still a long way from her potential earning plateau. Not one of the world's most powerful witches. She wasn't sure where the Season of her imagination might live—a gingerbread house or a crumbling castle surrounded by thorn trees, maybe. The yard of this cottage was dried out, mostly dirt with a few hardy weeds, but no thorn trees. The only thing she saw that suggested Season at all was over the door, where a small bundle of greenery had been tacked.

"Is that a charm of some kind?" Kerry asked. "Above the door?"

"Keeps us out," Daniel explained. "It's a ward."

"Really?" Kerry couldn't keep the surprise out of her voice. "That little bunch of leaves can keep you out of a place?"

"It's not just the leaves," he said. They had passed the house now, but he kept looking at it until he couldn't see it anymore. "It's what they represent, how she prepared them, and the way she put them up. Those leaves, properly prepared and blessed, have the power of the trees behind them. Strong enough to stand through the ages, limber enough to survive wind, structured to use rain instead of being worn away by it. With her help, the power of the trees is transferred to the bundle, and then applied to the whole house. I could no more walk in there right now than I could step through a redwood tree."

"Somehow I didn't think a little thing like that would be beyond your abilities," Kerry said, mostly joking.

But Daniel took it seriously. "I didn't say it was," he rejoined. "It just takes some preparation."

Rebecca, Josh, Brandy, and Scott were assigned to keep an eye on the bungalow while that preparation took place. Kerry drove Daniel back to their apartment, way down in Imperial Beach, phone on his lap the whole way in case they called to say she was on the move again. But the phone remained quiet.

Kerry was uneasy about leaving the others behind. The fact that they didn't call was no consolation—what if Season had somehow caught them unaware and done the same to them that she'd done to Mace? She could have called them, but that could be the same as demonstrating a lack of trust in them. She would have felt much better if Daniel had been able to stay close. But that wasn't an option, he assured her. He had work to do, work that couldn't be done until he knew just what they were up against.

The first thing he did when they got into the apartment was to borrow her laptop, plug it into the phone line, and get on the Internet.

There he went to a Web site that provided satellite views of any address in hundreds of cities, and called up the location of Season's bungalow. "The photos aren't all that current," he said. "But they don't have to be. I just want to see the area, not try to spot her through the roof or anything."

When he had zoomed in as far as he was able to online, he gazed at the image for a while. It lost clarity as it got closer, Kerry noted. And they didn't have a printer, so all he could do, she figured, was to look at it on the screen. But he asked her to find a piece of blank paper, and she rummaged through her belongings until she did, a brief letter from her aunt Betty, written on only one side of the page. Daniel spread the paper out flat on the tabletop and then put his hands on the computer screen. He spoke a couple of words in a language that Kerry didn't know, and then touched the paper.

As if it had run through a color laser printer—*or as if by magic, more accurately*, Kerry thought—the image that had appeared on screen transferred to the paper. But looking at it more closely, she realized that it was much more distinct now, that somehow in transferring it, Daniel sharpened it. Now it could have been a photo taken from a few hundred feet up, if that, showing the bungalow, its yard, and the houses and streets around it in crisp detail.

She was astonished. "If you could patent that, you could give Microsoft a run for its money."

Daniel shook his head. "Witches have gone up against Bill Gates before. He still wins. We're not all-powerful, you know."

He turned back to the image he'd made, and studied it. A couple of times he pointed out features to Kerry—the way the fence at the back of her place was leaning in one spot, suggesting weak support posts there; the fact that a neighbor's house behind hers was unfenced so that there was access to Emerald through that property. He traced his finger across the picture like a general planning a military campaign, which Kerry figured wasn't too far from the truth. For the most part, though, he was silent, working through details in his head without sharing them. Kerry knew that if he wanted to share, he would, and that quiet contemplation was probably more important right now.

When he finished with the picture, he excused himself and went into the room he shared with Josh. "I'll be in here for about twenty minutes," he said. "Don't come in, no matter what you might see or hear. I'll be fine. What I'm going to do isn't dangerous, but it's necessary, and it might sound unpleasant from the outside."

He gave Kerry a last kiss and closed the door. She crossed her arms in front of her chest and stood by the open front window, grateful for whatever breeze slipped through. The apartment was just small enough to be stuffy on these hot days, and though they got a decent cross breeze at night, during the day the air outside wasn't much of a relief. *I always heard San Diego was supposed to have perfect weather,* she thought. She had found out, though, that while it was mostly pleasant, it was far from perfect. She'd learned about June gloom, during which the beaches stayed socked in by overcast skies most of the day, so travelers who had come from far away for the fabled southern California coastline were disappointed by gray, cool days. July had been about as good as it gets, with warm, sunny weather all the time. Even August had started nice, but these last few days had reminded her that San Diego is essentially a desert, albeit one close to the ocean. She hadn't seen a drop of precipitation all summer, which cemented that impression.

Musing on the climate was just one way she tried to ignore the sounds that issued from Daniel's room. The first noises she heard were just strange—deep-sounding bells, like cowbells or heavy wind chimes, with a low moaning sound twining through them. But the sounds quickly became more disturbing—the moan less like wind, more like human voices, then turning to a keening wail, a mourning sound. When Daniel's voice entered the chorus, in evident agony, Kerry started to rush for the door. Remembering his warning, she kept herself from throwing it open, but it took every ounce of will power. She went back to the window.

When he screamed again, she turned away and crossed to the bathroom, running water full force in the sink, wetting a washcloth and laying it over her face. She pressed the corners against her ears, trying to keep all noise out, to amplify the blood she could hear in her own head, drowning out everything else.

Finally he emerged. He looked like he'd been through hell. His cheeks were drawn and pale, with red splotches on them. His eyes were glassy and unfocused. It looked like he might have blow-dried his hair in a wind tunnel. Kerry went to him and grabbed his hands, which were clammy. "Are you okay, Daniel? What happened in there?"

"I'm fine," he replied. His voice was a dry rasp that sounded like it reached her from some faraway place.

"But . . . what . . . ?" She didn't even know how to finish the question. It was obvious to her that she needed to know more about this whole business before she would know what to ask. He tugged absently at his hands, and Kerry released them.

"Another time," Daniel said. Already he seemed to be improving: color flooding back into his face, eyes clearing. He ran a hand over his head, smoothing the flyaway hair. Now he looked at her, really seeing her for the first time, she thought, since he'd come out of the room, and he smiled. "I'll tell you all about it later," he said. "It's just . . . preparations that have to be made. A little easier if I could have made them over the span of several days, as they should be. But since we didn't know precisely when battle might be joined, I had to hold off." He leaned forward, kissed her forehead. "You okay?"

"I'm . . . I'm not the one who was screaming in pain."

"Is that what you heard?" he asked. Kerry nodded her head, but Daniel didn't elaborate. "Let's go," he said. "We have a wicked witch to kill."

20

"Have you ever been in love, Kerry?" Daniel asked as he drove north on I-5, back toward Pacific Beach and the confrontation they both knew was imminent. "I mean, totally and completely head over heels?" Her heart leapt at the question. *Where is this going?* she wondered. She knew where she hoped he was taking the conversation. She had decided that—lack of personal experience with the emotion aside—she believed she was in love with Daniel. She couldn't stop thinking about him, worrying about him when he was away from her. She wanted to be with him every moment, wanted to feel his hands on her, his lips, the comfortable way they fit together when they walked or stood together, her weight on him and vice versa. There had been a hole in her life, and that hole had been Daniel-sized and Daniel-shaped, and now there was a Daniel in it.

She recognized that she was letting her silence last an awkwardly long time. "No. Never before." She hadn't wanted to come right out and say it, but figured that her reply was ambiguous enough to leave plenty of room for his own interpretation.

"Season was, once," he said simply. Kerry was stunned by the comment, which was so totally opposite from where she had hoped he was leading. "I killed him."

"You did?" was all she could manage.

He sat in silence for a moment, guiding the car up the busy freeway. "That's right. He was a witch—not a terribly powerful or influential one, not in her league or mine, definitely. But probably a nice enough guy, with a few talents of his own. He fell into her sphere of influence somehow, and . . . well, you've seen her. She is a very beautiful woman."

"Yes," Kerry had to agree. "She is that."

Daniel laughed. "Not in your league, of course. But beautiful just the same."

Kerry felt her cheeks warming. The thing

was, she got the impression he really did feel that way. He wasn't just saying it. When he looked at her and that smile illuminated his features, he seemed to be looking at something glorious, radiant. He could have been admiring one of the world's great pieces of art. But it was Kerry he was looking at. Just Kerry.

"Anyway, he fell in love with her almost at first glance, I guess. I only pieced it all together later, from things I heard. She came to return the feeling, and after a while—this is about two hundred years ago, I guess, in the early nineteenth century—she was as hopelessly in love with him as he was with her. They were together for a decade or so, completely wrapped up in each other. It was kind of sweet to see, but it made her weak. Distracted. Almost like she forgot we were out there, Abraham and I, looking for her."

There was really nothing Kerry could say to this, so she just tried to pay attention while her thoughts thundered along at a thousand miles an hour. *Is this a brush-off?* she wondered. *Is he telling me that he can't afford a relationship, that it's too dangerous, too distracting?*

"We found her in Philadelphia, in summer.

It was hot, like this, but humid, too, I remember. Thunderstorms in the afternoons that sounded like the world was falling apart around us. She and her lover—his name was Caleb—had taken a suite of rooms in a fine hotel. But they went out at night, became part of the social scene, and of course stories spread and people talked about the beautiful stranger, and we heard about it. When we got to Philadelphia we watched the hotel for a few days, saw them coming and going, learned their routine. That was what did them in: the routine they had developed."

The freeway exit loomed, but Daniel was so involved in his story, so lost in the past, that he almost missed it. When he noticed the exit, he ticked down the turn signal and darted across three lanes of roadway, just making it.

"Sorry," he said, sounding sheepish. "What was I saying about distraction? It's a dangerous thing."

"I guess it is," Kerry agreed, a little glum.

"We're almost there so I'll make this short," he continued. "Shorter, at least. Abraham and I came to know when they would be in and when they wouldn't. One night we waited until after they had left and then we went in, enchanted the hotel staff, let ourselves into their suite. We waited. We were ready for battle, but Season . . . Season had been making love, not war, for ten years. We knew we could defeat her.

"When they came back to the room, we were ready and they were utterly surprised. Shocked. I still smile when I think about the look on her face, that beautiful face with the blue eyes so wide, the brows raised, the mouth gaping open, lip quivering. Then rage set in. And Abraham and I attacked, both at once, as we'd planned. Season and Caleb both raised defensive shields, but Caleb's wasn't strong enough. Like Season, he was out of fighting fettle, soft and complacent." Daniel's tone changed, became quieter, with an edge that sounded almost bitter, Kerry thought. "I tore him in half without even thinking about it. Literally. Cut him apart at the waist. When his torso slid off his legs and fell to the floor, I could see Season changing in front of me. She hardened, right there, as if the last decade had never happened. She turned ferocious, throwing everything she had at us. We had believed it'd be a rout, but she turned out to be far more formidable than we'd expected, especially with the fury of a love lost powering her."

"Can't really blame her for that," Kerry opined. "I'd be really ticked if . . ." She let the sentence hang, unfinished.

He didn't seem to notice, though. He let go of one hand and fingered the scar on his jaw. "From someplace she drew an enchanted blade, and she pushed—physically pushed, like someone walking through water—her way past the spells I was casting at her, and she cut me with the knife. That put me out of the fight. I was in agony, losing blood, weak—any mortal would have been dead. I went down, passed out, I guess. Meanwhile she finished up with Abraham.

"When I came to"—His voice was tight now, his eyes narrowed to slits—"Abraham was dead. In pieces, like Caleb, only more of them. It looked like she had done it fast—a few slashing blows, one that cut off his right arm at the elbow, one across the left thigh, one at his throat. I must have appeared dead to her already—not surprising, really, since I was covered in blood, and my neck was cut wide open. I woke up in a hotel suite that was drenched in blood, with the remains of my brother and Caleb scattered around me, a knife on the ground, no Season in sight, and hotel personnel staring at me. One of the men vomited on the spot, and another ran to call the police. I was wanted for decades in Philadelphia after that—probably still am, since there's no statute of limitations on murder, but it's not like anyone is still expecting to find me.

"Things got more personal between us, after that," he went on. "Season and me, I mean. I had killed someone she loved; she had done the same to me, and nearly finished me as well. However inadvertently, she had framed me for the brutal murder of my own brother. I had always hated her, thanks to my mother's stories, but now the depth of my emotion changed. I didn't just want her dead; I wanted to tear her apart with my bare hands, piece by piece, glorying in the expression of sheer agony on her face while I did it. You've heard the cliché about wanting to dance on someone's grave. I want more than that—I want to dance on her body while it's still steaming, still bloody and warm."

Daniel made the turn onto Emerald. Season's house was less than a block away. The conversational thread was worrying Kerry—instead of leading up to Daniel confessing some kind of deep feelings for her, he was, frankly, freaking her out with his talk of bloody revenge. She supposed he was steeling himself for the battle at hand, preparing himself by remembering the reasons for it. But she didn't like it at all.

He braked the car around the corner from Season's bungalow, behind Scott's RAV4, in the shade of a jacaranda tree. "Sorry, I didn't mean this to be so grim," he said as he shut off the engine. "What I really meant to say, Kerry, is that I don't want to see anything happen to you today. I don't want to repeat what happened to Season and Caleb. Now that I've found you . . . I don't want to lose you, Kerry. Ever."

Well, that's better, Kerry thought. *Not quite a declaration of undying love, but close enough for now.* She leaned over and kissed him on the cheek before she opened her door. The doors of the RAV4 opened at the same time, and Scott and Brandy stepped out. Even from the sidewalk, Kerry could feel the heat radiating from the blacktop. She blinked against the sun and scorching air.

"She's still in there," Scott reported. "Unless she's got teleportation technology or something. We've been on this end, and Josh and Rebecca are parked on the other. She hasn't budged."

"Season has a lot of talents," Daniel said seriously. "Teleportation is not, to my knowledge, one of them."

"Then she's in there," Scott reiterated. "How do we get her out?"

Daniel shook his head. "*We* don't," he said forcefully. "I take it from here."

Brandy wagged a finger at him. "You got us into this, mister," she declared. "You can't just shut us out of it now."

Daniel's gaze flitted from one to the other, and even down the block where Kerry knew Rebecca and Josh were waiting for the word. "This is where it gets well and truly dangerous," Daniel said. "Deadly. I don't want you guys anywhere near here. You've done your part, and then some. Today Season Howe dies, and you can all go about the rest of your lives knowing that you've done a good thing, you've saved people you'll never meet."

Except we couldn't even save Mace, Kerry thought. "I think we want more than that, Daniel," she told him. "I know I do. After what we've been through, we want to be there for the end. We want to see Season finished, with our own eyes. We want to help if we can."

Brandy nodded, smiling. "Bulldog's got that right."

Scott didn't look as convinced, but as usual he was willing to go along with Brandy. "It's unanimous," he announced.

"What about Josh and Rebecca?" Daniel asked. "They can still get out of here if they want to."

"You'd have to ask them," Scott replied. He handed his cell phone to Daniel. "But I have a feeling I know what they'll say."

Daniel declined the phone, but used his own and called the other two. They walked down the street and around the corner, joining the rest of the group. Kerry felt pleased that they were all together for this—all except Mace, of course, but he wouldn't have wanted anything to do with it anyway. She thought it was important, though, for reasons she couldn't even really enumerate, that they be absolutely unanimous on this one.

As it turned out, they were.

Once the vote had been made clear, Daniel relented and outlined his plan. As soon as he started describing it, Kerry realized that he had expected them to want to take part from the very beginning—that the finger-tracing he'd done on his self-printed aerial photo had taken all of them into account, not just himself. She should have known he couldn't be in all of those places at once. As he'd said of Season, he had many talents, but some things were beyond even his abilities.

Five minutes later, everyone was on the move.

21

Kerry didn't have as far to go as most of the rest. Daniel had pointed out a big red SUV halfway down the short block, almost directly in front of Season's house but across the street, and instructed her to go sit on the ground behind it—right at the rear wheels, so Season wouldn't see her feet beneath the vehicle. Scott and Brandy hopped back in the RAV4 and drove past Season's place, then around the block. An alley bisected the block, lengthwise. Because Season's place was on the short connecting block between the main streets of Emerald and Felspar, the alley ran beside the fence enclosing her yard. They parked the car and got out, positioning themselves so they could see the whole line of Season's back fence. If she tried to run, they'd see her.

Not that they could stop her, at least not for long. But, as Daniel pointed out, all they had to do was slow her down.

It was, they all knew, potentially the most dangerous thing they'd ever attempted. Kerry found herself swallowing, again and again, as if her terror was something stuck in her throat. But it wouldn't go away. She felt cold and raw, like she'd been through a punishing hailstorm.

When Brandy and Scott were in place, a quick cell phone call alerted the others. Daniel started Rebecca and Josh on their way—what Josh called the Long Walk—down the block to take up positions at the front corners of Season's yard. While they walked, Daniel tossed Kerry a grin, blew her a kiss, and went to take his own position on the far side of a gray sedan parked on the street in front of the house next to Season's, on the corner of Emerald and Everts. Like Kerry, he ducked down behind the car, hidden from Season's view by the wheels. The dark sky of gloaming made hiding all the easier.

When they were all in position, Daniel gave Rebecca and Josh the high sign. Standing at the corners of her yard, they began to call her name. "Season," they chanted. "Season Howe."

Hearing the chant begin, Brandy and Scott picked it up at the rear of the house. Within moments, all four were calling in unison. "Season. Season Howe."

"When she hears her name, she'll scan you from inside the house," Daniel had warned them. "She'll know that you don't have any magical abilities, though. I'm counting on her being too curious to resist checking you out further, to see what's going on, how you know who she is. She'll come outside."

Apparently Daniel knew her well. Kerry couldn't see what was going on—she was under strict orders not to make any part of herself visible to Season—but at one point, shortly after the four-part harmony kicked in, she thought Josh's voice caught, and then a moment later Rebecca's did the same. *She's scanning them,* Kerry realized with dismay, *and they can feel it. Feel her digging around inside them. Ick.*

The chanting continued for another thirty seconds or so. Kerry had been worried that other neighbors would freak out at this undeniably odd behavior, and call the police or interfere themselves. Daniel had assured her that it wouldn't be a problem, and she hadn't been anxious for him to elaborate on that.

So when she heard a door open and then close, she was pretty sure that it was Season. Doubly so when she heard the woman's voice.

"Who are you? What do you want?"

She would, Daniel had warned, be on full alert when she came outside. She would obviously know that something was going on, that her cover had been blown, but at first she wouldn't know why and by whom. The key to taking her was to keep her off guard, keep her wondering just what was happening, and not to let her raise the proper defense in time.

Now she was outside, though, and that was Kerry's cue. She could barely get her legs to cooperate, and her hands were shaking like crazy, flopping around like two fish on a line. But finally she got her appendages in order and emerged from behind the SUV. When she spoke, her voice even surprised her with the authority she managed to put into it.

"We're here for you, Season Howe," she said. "We know who you are. We know what you are. And we're here to make sure this is your last day on Earth."

The witch was standing on her front porch. Now, she turned to face Kerry. A storm of emotion washed across Season's beautiful face. A moment of shock when she recognized Kerry, or at least a realization that she had seen her before. That was followed by amusement, when, Kerry believed, she understood that she was being called out by five powerless mortals who hadn't even come bearing traditional weapons much less mystical ones. Kerry was gratified by what looked like a moment of doubt, as if she was second-guessing herself, wondering if these five were as powerless as they looked, because if they were, how would they have dared to confront her?

But her face settled into anger, clouded and red, as she regarded Kerry across the street. "I know you," she said, her voice quaking with rage. "You . . . you were with him. With Daniel Blessing."

"That's right," Kerry answered. This part hadn't been scripted, and she was winging it. But she felt emboldened by Season's anger—

the witch wouldn't be so mad if she wasn't concerned, she figured.

And she has every reason to be concerned.

Season stepped down from her porch, beckoning Kerry with one crooked finger. "Come here," she commanded. "I want to talk to you."

Kerry maintained her position next to the SUV, so she could duck behind it for cover at any moment. She didn't have to wait long, though. As soon as Season's shoe clicked on the sidewalk in front of her house, Daniel made his move.

He rose up from behind the gray car like a jack-in-the-box. Spoke one of the words that Kerry still couldn't understand, but which Daniel had told her were in an incredibly ancient tongue, long since forgotten by most humans. Made a hurling motion with both hands, toward Season, who only now noticed his presence. Again, her expression changed rapidly, rotating through a variety of emotions—surprise, fear, fury—in the space of a quarter second.

That was all the time she had.

Formed from empty air, picking up apparent mass and force as it went, Daniel's spell had created, manifested, or otherwise brought into being a roiling ball of pure energy. At least that's what it looked like to Kerry's admittedly untutored eye. Transparent, it seemed to warp the view behind it, like how heat shimmers the scenery on a summer day. She could only see its outline by watching where the background was clear and where it wavered and shifted.

Season barely had time to register it before the energy ball struck her, with a sound like a thunderclap.

The force of the impact drove her to her knees, blasting her hair like a hurricane wind, shredding her blouse. When it was past she glared up at Daniel with fire in her eyes, a thin trickle of blood running from the corner of her mouth.

And another one hit her, laying her out on her back.

Season swore, scrabbled to turn over, to regain her footing. The next one slammed into her before she could stand steadily, but when she went down this time, it was on her stomach.

Daniel kept up the attack. Kerry watched in dumfounded horror. The destructive potential contained inside Daniel had always been theoretical to her—potential, not actual. Seeing it at work was terrifying. She knew it was for the best possible reasons, knew it had to be done.

But that didn't make it easy to watch.

Daniel changed weapons now. Instead of the roiling energy balls, he spoke different words of the ancient language, and bolts of violet lightning seemed to issue from his fingertips, blasting at Season like the weapons of Zeus. Where they struck her, her clothing tore, her skin smoldered.

Still, she lived.

Still, she fixed Daniel Blessing with a murderous glare.

She hadn't had a chance since he had launched his attack to counterattack. He had never let up, not for a moment. His plan, simple as it was, had worked to the letter.

Season Howe was finished, Kerry thought. Daniel had fulfilled his lifelong goal.

Finally, after what seemed an unbearably long and torturous assault, Season was still.

She lay on the walkway leading up to her front steps. Blood streaked the pale cement. Her body looked, in the pale remnants of daylight, as if it had lost an endurance contest with a threshing machine: cuts and tears everywhere, clothing ribboned.

Kerry started toward her, but Daniel waved her away. She glanced around her, saw that Brandy and Scott had come around from the back and joined Rebecca and Josh in the street. Brandy's eyes were wide and glittering with fear—at last, Kerry understood, even she believed what the rest already accepted. Kerry would go stand with them, she decided, and wait for Daniel's all clear.

It never came.

Season was dead, anyone could see that. She'd stopped moving long before, except for involuntary motions, her body buffeted about by the force of Daniel's attack. Even then, he had not let up. Finally she was as limp as BoBo, the rag-doll clown Kerry had slept with from the time she was three until after her mother got sick, when Kerry had decided it was time to grow up, to stop playing with toys, because she was the only functional person left in the house.

Still, Daniel approached her with caution. Stood a dozen feet from her and watched the body, looking for any sign of breath, of life. Satisfied, he moved closer. Stopped, watched again. Closer.

Finally crouched over her. Touched her shoulder, rocking her over, onto her back, and releasing.

Limp. Lifeless.

Kerry knew Daniel by now, knew him well enough to recognize the look of relief that washed across his face. Relief, and something else.

Accomplishment. He had done it. *They* had done it—distracted her, made her forget to look for the real threat.

Daniel locked eyes with Kerry, smiling. Kerry tried to look into those eyes, from this distance, tried to tell him with her own gaze that she loved him. That she always had, somehow, from that first night. That she always would.

So neither one of them noticed that the witch moved her hand—just a simple move, really, a flick of the wrist, almost casual. An observer might have thought it was a post-mortem reflex.

But it wasn't. There was purpose behind it.

Season's lips moved at the same time, uttering an ancient phrase of her own.

And Season's attack, at such close range—even through her own pain, her own seeming defeat—was devastating.

One second Kerry was looking into Daniel's gray eyes and the next, those eyes were scrunched shut, his face twisted in agony, his knees buckling. *Oh, no,* Kerry thought, but the rest of her thought was wordless, just fear piled upon horror upon the misery of seeing the man she loved brought down by a sudden, treacherous blow.

Season moved again, not much more than a twitch—this time, Kerry watched her, a soundless scream on her lips—and again, Daniel was wracked with pain. He fell to his hands and knees in Season's yard, still facing away from her, toward Kerry. His head hung down toward the lawn but he raised it, his gaze meeting Kerry's once again, holding it, and he was trying to mouth something to her when Season struck a third time.

The last time.

Season managed to push herself to her own knees now, and clearly she wasn't dead, after all—should have been, anyone else would have been, but not her. Her face contorted in rage and she moved both hands this time, mouth speaking words Kerry couldn't even hear over the thunderous roar that accompanied her motion, and Daniel—

Kerry tried to focus on his eyes, those warm, loving eyes, not on the rest of it.

—and Daniel let out a last cry, a wail of loss and longing, as Season's blast crushed him like a squirrel under the wheel of a semitruck. His body collapsed, his spine splintered, his limbs suddenly giving out, blood jetting in every direction, landing with a wet splatter like a lawn sprinkler. His eyes shone for a brief moment and then closed, and with a final shudder he fell onto the grass.

And Season stood, rose up to her full height, fists clenched, face still showing traces of anger but also something else, something that looked like sorrow, and she ignored the others huddled in the street, looking only at Kerry.

Kerry swallowed. Season had defeated Daniel—*killed Daniel,* she corrected herself, she never wanted to let go of that knowledge.

She would never forgive Season for that. But at the same time, she didn't exactly want Season to unleash that power against her.

Season didn't. Instead she spoke words Kerry could comprehend, though it took her a few moments to track them, to realize what the witch was saying to her.

"This is done now," Season said, without preamble. "This was between me and Daniel Blessing. At long last, it's over. He lost. I won. That's all there is to it. Go now, and don't concern yourselves any longer with issues far beyond your ken. Know that I could easily do to you as I did to him, but I'm not. I won't. Just go."

"But . . . ," Kerry began. "You . . . you killed him."

"As he very nearly did me." Season crossed her arms defiantly across her chest. "Go. Before I lose patience."

"He . . ." Kerry felt hands on her arm. Rebecca's voice whispered to her.

"Kerry, for God's sake let's get out of here. You saw—"

"I saw."

"—what she did to Daniel. We can't fight her. Come on."

"But . . ."

"She's right," Josh said. "This is lose-lose. Cut your losses and let's go."

Now there were other hands on her, tugging on her. In her yard, standing over Daniel's lifeless form, Season nodded her head. She looked almost sympathetic now, as if she understood what Kerry was feeling.

Maybe she did. Kerry remembered the story Daniel had told, just a few minutes ago, really, about Caleb. The one man Season had loved.

Maybe she'd just had her long-delayed revenge for that.

Well, Kerry thought, *revenge can go two ways.* She let the hands tug her away, toward the waiting car.

Away from Daniel, and Season.

Her eyes filled with tears, her heart with sorrow.

Daniel . . .

I'm writing this at 33,000 feet, scrunched into the window seat of a 737, nonstop from San Diego to Chicago. The guy next to me is snoring, his bulk slopping over the armrest into my space. It's a red-eye, of course—only appropriate, given my bloodshot, puffy peepers. The plan is to meet Aunt Betty and Uncle Marsh in Chicago, then spend a couple of days there together before I go on to Northwestern. I'm hoping that we'll be able to fill the days—Field Museum, shopping on the Miracle Mile, pizza at Gino's East, coffee in Wicker Park, etc.—enough so that B & M won't fight with each other, or me, too much.

I called Aunt Betty and asked her to bring a few things from the house with her, most especially BoBo the clown. I'm feeling the need for some comforting, some retreat, some healing. Hoping he can help with that.

It took us a couple of days to get past what had happened enough to clear out of the apartment and separate. Josh off to UNLV, Rebecca to UC Santa Cruz, Scott and Brandy beginning the long cross-country drive back to Harvard. And me, on a plane to O'Hare, and a life that suddenly feels like someone else's, not at all like the me I expected, a month ago, to see sitting on that plane in the dark. In my suitcase, along with my clothes and a couple of personal things, are Daniel's journals, all of them that I could find, anyway. And the letter.

Oh yeah, the letter.

It was on my pillow when I got home, that night. It had not been there when I left the apartment—I was in the bedroom last, and Daniel didn't go in at all after coming out from his "preparations" in his room. So, no letter then.

But letter after. Go figure. Daniel has his ways.

It's not long, and of course I've read it so many times it's committed to memory. But considering the way it came into being, who knows when it might vanish again? So I'll put it down here, and if I have a word or two wrong I'll correct it later.

Dearest Kerry,

I liked the way that looked, and read it several times, right off the bat. Even spoke the words out loud, much to Rebecca's surprise. Plus, I was not looking forward to the rest of it, since I was pretty convinced it wasn't good news.

Dearest Kerry,
If you see this letter, it means I did not beat

Season after all, and that she destroyed me. If you had to watch that—and, knowing you, I'm guessing you did; certain I couldn't dissuade you if you had put your mind to it—I am sorrier than you will ever know.

It was, of course, never my intent to involve you in this whole business. My fight, not yours, and all of that. Still, since we were thrown together, by fate or whatever you might choose to name it, I am proud and honored that you chose to throw in your lot with me.

But now it's over for you. I know you'll be angry at Season, and sad to have lost me, but please, please don't get it into your head that you can somehow avenge my death. I think I told you once that Season is quite possibly the most powerful of us. I had a chance, though a slim one, and apparently not a good enough one. You wouldn't. You are a remarkable woman, wise and mature and breathtakingly lovely, but you wouldn't last ten seconds against Season Howe.

So put this summer's experiences into your box of memories. Treasure the brief time we had together. Mourn me for a short while, and then get on with the rest of your life. It will be an incredible adventure, and I only wish I could be there to share it with you.

Death, Kerry, is not the end. It's a passage, a

process. In some fashion I will be forever with you, and you will always be a part of me.

In life, though I never said it—I didn't want you to feel any obligation to me, and I knew that our time together might be short and end brutally—I loved you. In death, I love you still.

So, forward! Aspire! Achieve!

I remain,

Daniel Blessing

Yeah . . . so what do you do with that?

Captain just announced that he's beginning our descent. In another few minutes, laptops will have to be put away, tray tables stowed, and all that stuff. Then Aunt Betty and Uncle Marsh will be there, and then college. Endings, beginnings. Passages.

More later.

K.

End of Book One

As the seasons change, so does Kerry. . . .
Check out this excerpt from the next

witch
season

FALL

Mother Blessing was a surprise.

Kerry had begun to think she'd never find Daniel Blessing's mother. The Great Dismal was just too big, too dense, too full of dangers. She saw a black bear her first morning out; fortunately the bear saw her and turned back the way he had come, vanishing down a trail that seemed too narrow for a human, much less a huge furry beast. She had barely reined in her galloping heart when the creek before her, wider now and flowing faster than when it had merely been a ditch that ran alongside the old town site, parted and an alligator drifted to the surface a few feet ahead of her. Kerry had a quick mental picture of it tearing into her inflatable boat with its razored teeth and sinking her, then finishing her off at its leisure. *This was a bad idea,* she thought, *a stupendously bad idea in a lifetime chock full of bad ideas.*

"I taste bad!" she shouted at the beast. "Really bad! That's what everyone tells me, anyway. Kerry, you taste bad. And you smell funny too."

Apparently she was convincing enough, because the gator drifted past her without biting her boat. For a couple of hours after that, she started to get used to the swamp, even to enjoy it. Tall trees arced over her head, creating an effect like a green cathedral. The fragrant forest floor was festooned with wide-leaf ferns. Butterflies and birds flitted and flew; squirrels scampered up the sides of trees; great multi-hued spiders spun webs like fishnets between tree trunks. There was a quiet charm to the place that she appreciated in a way she would never have expected the night before, when she had been so afraid that she had barely managed to sleep at all.

The swamp had turned cool during the

night and Kerry had snuggled into her sleeping bag, listening to the crickets and frogs and other, stranger night noises. This morning she had crawled out, still wearing the same jeans and fleece sweatshirt she'd worn the day before. She brushed her teeth by the edge of the water, rinsing with bottled water, but felt grungy from lack of a shower. As the day wore on, her nearly-sleepless night began to catch up with her, and the beauty of the swamp combined with the gentle motion of the boat to lull her into a kind of stupor. So when she first noticed the men watching her from the banks, she didn't think anything of it. After a couple of minutes, she realized that there was something wrong about it—that men shouldn't watch her here, that she was unique enough in a place like this that any other human would hail her, not simply observe from the cover of thick underbrush. She tried to focus on the spot where she thought she'd seen one of them, but he was gone. Maybe a leaf shuddered slightly with his passing, or maybe it was a wisp of a breeze that moved it.

But Kerry was on the alert now, wide awake, senses sharpened. If she saw anything else she'd be ready.

Or so she thought.

The creek forked, and Kerry chose the right course. But though she paddled that way, the current had another idea, and it pushed her toward the left. She thought she remembered something in the journals about the right fork, and tried to fight the pull of the creek. She lost the struggle, though, and gave it up after a few minutes, concentrating on keeping the boat steady against the sudden surge, trying not to capsize, instead of worrying about which fork she should take when, for all practical purposes, she had no idea where she was or where she should be.

Just when she had the little boat settled on the water, Kerry caught another glimpse of movement through the thick trees. For a moment she thought it was a deer, or maybe— her heart pounded in fear—another bear. *What are you supposed to do in the event of a bear attack?* she tried to remember. *Make noise? Play dead? Run like hell?* Making noise seemed like the easiest, especially since trying to run might involve drowning, or a close-up encounter with an alligator or a water moccasin. For a moment she thought maybe she'd be okay if she stayed in the boat and it was on land, but then she remembered pictures of bears standing in rushing rivers, fishing for lunch. *So much for that idea.*

She brought the little paddle up out of the water and laid it across the boat's stern, trying to sit very still to minimize any sound. Maybe it hadn't noticed her at all. Through the trees, another flash of motion—something big and dark, it seemed—caught her eye. This time she heard a noise, too, a rustling of leaves.

So it's not just shifting shadows.

As quietly as she could, she slipped the paddle back into the water and rowed for the opposite bank. The banks on both sides were sheer, with trees right to the edge, roots erupting from the cutaways. She wasn't sure where she'd be able to climb out of the boat, but she wanted to at least have a chance if some creature came at her.

The foliage across the water shifted again, as if something with serious weight came through it in her direction. That was all it took to spur Kerry. With two more powerful sweeps of the oar she made the far bank. There was a rope tied to a ring at the boat's bow, and she quickly looped it around the root of a tree. Then, setting her feet widely for best balance, she stood, clutching at a narrow trunk for more support. Putting one foot up on the bank, she hoisted herself from the boat and slid between two trees just as the dark figure on the far shore loomed into view.

It was not a bear, but a man.

Everything she'd read about the Great Dismal rushed back into her consciousness: a haven for criminals, runaway slaves before the Civil War and Emancipation, and hunters and fishers. If the man across the way had innocent intent he'd have said something by now, surely, not approached her with stealth and silence.

The ground under her feet was soft and spongy, the trees close together, with ferns and trailing vines covering the lower reaches and tangles of thickets tearing at her legs. Placing her feet was difficult, but she didn't intend just to stand there and let someone sneak up on her. As fast as she could manage, she pushed her way through the underbrush and around the trees, putting distance between herself and the creek. Once she had a rhythm going, she was able to get up a reasonable speed.

She was going so quickly, in fact, that she didn't at first notice the dark man who stood in front of her. When she did, it was too late;

he swung something heavy at her and she tried to dodge, but a tree trunk blocked her way. A flash of light accompanied the impact, and then everything went dark.

I have to be dreaming, Kerry thought. *This can't be real.*

She seemed to be in an actual bed, with crisp, clean sheets pulled up around her. A dull ache throbbed at her right temple, but it wasn't any worse than an average headache, and there was none of the nausea she might have expected, given the fact that she had apparently been clubbed into unconsciousness. The odors around her—she hadn't yet opened her eyes— were clean, almost antiseptic, not the pungent aroma of the swamp.

And there were two exceedingly strange sounds: one a kind of electrical hum, and one a labored, artificial breathing noise, as if Darth Vader stood beside the bed holding a small appliance.

Or a light saber.

Having gathered as much (seemingly contradictory) information as possible, Kerry opened her eyes.

The first thing she saw was a woman—an

enormous woman who looked to be in her fifties or sixties, big in every way, from her teased, bleached, beehive of a hairdo, to her vast bosom and belly, barely confined in a plaid smock the size of a pup tent, to the thighs straining royal blue polyester stretch pants—smiling at her from a motorized scooter/wheelchair, a clear plastic mask across her nose and mouth attached by tubes to oxygen tanks mounted on the scooter's rear. The scooter had wide rubber tires and a shallow basket mounted on the handlebars.

"Welcome back, darlin'," the woman said, her Southern accent thick as the trees in the Great Dismal. "I've been wonderin' when you'd be joinin' me. I'm so sorry for the way my boys brought you here."

"Here?" Kerry essayed weakly.

"My house, of course," the woman replied. "Y'all were lookin' for me, weren't you?"

Kerry tried to raise herself up on one elbow. "You . . . you're . . ."

The woman breathed loudly into her mask, and then favored Kerry with another broad, slightly grotesque smile. "Folks call me Mother Blessing."

JEFF MARIOTTE is the author of more than fifteen previous novels, including several set in the universes of Buffy the Vampire Slayer, Angel, Charmed, and Star Trek; the original horror novel *The Slab;* and more comic books than he has time to count, some of which have been nominated for Stoker and International Horror Guild Awards. With his wife Maryelizabeth Hart and partner Terry Gilman, he co-owns Mysterious Galaxy, a bookstore specializing in science fiction, fantasy, mystery, and horror.

He lives with his family and pets in San Diego, California, in a home filled with books, music, toys, and other examples of American pop culture. More information than you would ever want to know about him can be found at www.jeffmariotte.com.

As many as 1 in 3 Americans
who have HIV... don't know it.

TAKE CONTROL.
KNOW YOUR STATUS.
GET TESTED.

To learn more about HIV testing,
or get a free guide to HIV and
other sexually transmitted diseases:

www.knowhivaids.org
1-866-344-KNOW

the nine lives of chloe king

by CELIA THOMSON

**1 hero.
9 lives.
8 left.**

It happened fast. Just a moment earlier, Chloe had been sitting with Amy and Paul on the observation deck atop Coit Tower in San Francisco. *What would happen if I dropped a penny from up here?* she wondered. She climbed up on the railing and dug into her jeans pocket, hunting for spare change.

That was when she fell.

As Chloe tumbled through the fog, all she could think was, *My mother will be so upset when she finds out I skipped school. . . . Maybe all that stuff about your life flashing before your eyes is just bull.*

Or maybe Chloe already knew, down in the unconscious depths of her mind, that she still had eight lives to go.

Don't miss this hot new series from Simon Pulse:

The Fallen

The Stolen

Published by Simon & Schuster